MARVELOUS
MARVIN

and the

Wolfman
Mystery

Weekly Reader Book Club Presents

MARVELOUS
MARVIN

and the

Wolfman
Mystery

Bonnie Pryor

illustrated by

Melissa Sweet

Morrow Junior Books New York

This book is a presentation of Newfield Publications, Inc .
Newfield Publications offers book clubs for children from
preschool through high school. For further information
write to: **Newfield Publications, Inc.,**
4343 Equity Drive, Columbus, Ohio 43228.

Published by arrangement with William Morrow and Company, Inc.
Newfield Publications is a federally registered trademark
of Newfield Publications, Inc.
Weekly Reader is a federally registered trademark
of Weekly Reader Corporation.

Monotype with mixed media were used for the illustrations.
The text type is 13-point Carmina Light/Bitstream.

Text copyright © 1994 by Bonnie Pryor
Illustrations copyright © 1994 by Melissa Sweet

Library of Congress Cataloging-in-Publication Data
Pryor, Bonnie.
Marvelous Marvin and the Wolfman Mystery/Bonnie Pryor;
illustrated by Melissa Sweet. p. cm.
Summary: Marvin looks for clues after suspecting that his new neighbor is a
werewolf and involved in a murder conspiracy.
ISBN 0-688-12866-1
[1. Mystery and detective stories.] I. Sweet, Melissa, ill. II. Title.
III. Title: Wolfman Mystery. PZ7.P94965Mar 1994
[Fic]—dc20 93-49686 CIP AC

To Corey Adam
—B.P.

To Carole and Dana
—M.S.

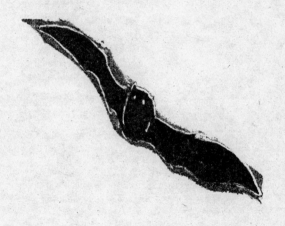

CONTENTS

MARVELOUS
MARVIN

and the

Wolfman
Mystery

ONE

Do Detectives
GO GROCERY
SHOPPING?

"I hate going shopping," Marvin groaned.

"You like to eat, don't you?" Mrs. Fremont asked cheerfully as she pulled the car into a parking place outside McNaulty's grocery store. There was a newer grocery store at the mall on the other side of Liberty Corners, but Mrs. Fremont preferred to go to a little shopping center not far from their house.

"Just because we like to eat doesn't mean we want to spend every Saturday morning in the grocery store." For once Marvin's twin sister, Sarah, was on his side. "We are probably the only kids in the whole world who have never seen Saturday morning cartoons."

"I rather doubt that." Their mother chuckled as she pointed to the crowded neighborhood store. "Saturday morning is the only time a lot of people can shop."

Mrs. Fremont worked all week at an insurance company, and Mr. Fremont's job at the bank required him to work Saturday mornings. The twins felt they were old enough to be left alone for more than a short time, but their mother disagreed. After school they stayed by themselves for the hour before she arrived home, but every Saturday morning she insisted they come with her. Sarah rolled her eyes at Marvin, but both of them knew it was useless to argue further—until the next week, at any rate.

Just as Mrs. Fremont was switching off the ignition, a shiny red sports car pulled into the next space. One of their neighbors, a friendly woman named Mrs. Hanson, opened the car door, pausing to pat her springy gray curls back into place.

"How do you like my new car?" she asked when she noticed the Fremonts staring.

"It's great," Marvin exclaimed.

"I always wanted one like this. Couldn't afford it when the kids were home." Mrs. Hanson patted a red fender. "It's my baby."

"I think it's wonderful," Mrs. Fremont said with a wistful look at her own sedate station wagon. Marvin wondered whether his mother would drive a red sports car when he was grown.

Sarah was walking around admiring the car. "Oh, jeepers, here's a little dent," she called from the passenger side. "Did somebody bump you?"

Mrs. Hanson looked sheepish. "No, I did it myself. Wouldn't you think it would be easy to park a little car like this without hitting something? But the garage has ordered a new bumper. In a couple of weeks it will be as good as new."

Inside McNaulty's, Mrs. Hanson pulled a cart from the line at the door and with a wave buzzed away. Mrs. Fremont took a cart for herself and started more slowly down the first aisle. The twins reluctantly followed.

Sarah went back to grumbling. "Grocery stores are so boring."

Mrs. Fremont examined a bag of yellow apples, looking for bruises. "It's good experience for you," she said in exasperation. "When you grow up, you will thank me for teaching you how to be a careful shopper."

"When I grow up, I'm never going to make my children spend Saturday morning in a grocery store," Sarah said.

"I'm never even going to the grocery store," Marvin told his mother. "I will be too busy catching criminals and bringing them to justice."

Sarah snorted. "That's what you want to do

this week? Last week you wanted to investigate UFO sightings. You are *so* weird." In spite of her words, she smiled at her brother. For all their differences they really got along very well.

People meeting Marvin and Sarah for the first time were always amazed that they were twins. In the first place, they didn't even look alike. Marvin was small for his age. He was quiet and could most often be found with his nose in a comic book. He wore glasses, which made him look more serious than he really was. Sarah was taller, although her hair was the same straight dark brown as Marvin's. She was usually busy with some project or other. Her latest interest was photography. She seldom went anywhere without her camera and was always studying ways to make better pictures.

"Even criminals have to eat," remarked Mrs. Fremont. "Maybe right this very minute there is a dastardly crook lurking about the tomatoes."

"Oh, Mom." Marvin sighed, knowing she was teasing. Just the same, he glanced quickly about. The only person at the tomato counter was old Mrs. Parson, who lived down the street—no mystery there. But farther down the aisle was the last person Marvin wanted to meet on a Saturday morning, or any other morning, for that matter.

TWO

A Strange CONVERSATION

Even shopping with his mother, Mean Ernie Farrow looked more like a tank than a fourth-grade boy. He swaggered past the milk counter, pushing his cart directly toward them. Marvin stepped behind his mother, wishing for a place to hide.

"Could we at least look at the magazines?" Sarah begged. She never worried about bullies who demanded desserts from your lunch and threatened to pound you to a pulp if you refused. "I'll go with her," Marvin offered quickly. He thought the magazine section was probably the safest place in the store to hide. Mean Ernie was more interested in bashing people than in reading.

Mrs. Fremont hesitated. "All right, but just for a minute. Then you catch up with me."

The magazines were kept in a little alcove

5

next to the rows of grocery carts as you entered the store. Marvin managed to slink back without being spotted. He picked up a comic book from the revolving rack and peeked over the top of a page just in case Ernie should suddenly appear. Sarah was soon engrossed in a magazine called *Darkroom Techniques*. She was learning how to develop her own photographs.

At last Marvin spotted Mean Ernie and his mother going through the checkout line. Marvin allowed himself to relax. He amused himself by watching other people who came into the store. Lately Marvin had been reading a lot of mystery stories. His favorites were the Hardy Boys. He knew from them that a good detective is always alert for peculiar behavior.

A woman entered the store, carrying a small child. She buckled her child into the grocery cart's seat. Marvin watched as she started through the rows of vegetable bins. The child was howling for a candy bar and grabbing at the packages of carrots stacked neatly on a shelf. The woman looked embarrassed rather than suspicious. Most mothers were too busy buying groceries to be very good criminals, Marvin decided.

Through the window Marvin watched

Frankie, the neighborhood handyman, drive up and park a shiny green convertible. Frankie was tall and skinny. His black hair was slicked back and looked dirty. Frankie was an unpleasant sort of person, and now, as usual, he was scowling. Marvin watched as the handyman walked right past the vegetables and started gathering an armload of soda pop and junk food. Marvin yawned. Saturdays were very boring.

Marvin started reading the comic book he was holding. It was called *Werewolf's Revenge*. According to the story, most of the time the werewolf was a quiet little man who looked just like everyone else. But when the moon was full, he turned into a wild beast. Marvin was soon so engrossed that he jumped when his mother tapped him on the arm.

"I left an envelope of coupons on the car seat," Mrs. Fremont said. "Would you mind running out and getting them for me?"

"Sure," Marvin said. He reluctantly replaced the comic book in the rack, squeezed past the grocery carts, and headed out the door.

Marvin was still thinking about *Werewolf's Revenge* as he wound his way through the rows of cars. Then suddenly he stopped. A man was getting out of his car at the end of the next row. He looked a little bit like the man in the werewolf story, Marvin thought to himself as he walked closer. Then suddenly Marvin realized who it was. It was his strange new neighbor, Mr. Wolfe.

Mr. Wolfe had moved next door only a month ago. The twins had hoped a family with children their age would move into the house. It certainly was large enough for a family. But Mr. Wolfe lived alone. The twins seldom saw him. Most of the day the house was silent and the shades were drawn. But late at night the lights were on, and the Fremonts could hear loud banging noises that continued far into the night.

Just as Mr. Wolfe shut his car door, another car whipped into the next parking space. A red-faced, heavyset man jumped out.

"I've been looking for you everywhere," he said. "Lucky I saw you pulling into this parking lot. I've got a message for you from Mr. Fiumera." The red-faced man waved his arms as he talked. "He's very worried that the job won't be done on schedule. He's especially concerned with the time you're spending on Henry."

"Just give me a few days more," Mr. Wolfe pleaded. "Believe me, it will be worth it."

"I'm sure it would be," the red-faced man said impatiently, "but we're facing a deadline. Mr. Fiumera wants you to eliminate Henry *now*."

Marvin stopped, frozen in his tracks. Every hair on his head seemed to stand straight up. He forced his feet to keep walking, pretending not to notice.

Mr. Wolfe's voice was quiet. Marvin had to strain to hear as he walked by. "I like Henry," he protested.

"We've got a contract." The other man's voice was loud and clear. "If Mr. Fiumera says to get rid of Henry, you'll have to do it. Mr. Fiumera likes the other one better, anyway." He handed Mr. Wolfe a paper. "Here's my home number. Call me when the job is done."

Marvin reached his mother's car. The men seemed to have noticed him for the first time. They stood silently, watching as he reached in the car and picked up his mother's coupons. Marvin's knees were shaking so hard, he was amazed his legs were holding him up. Mr. Wolfe smiled slightly and nodded, but Marvin did not return the smile. He raced across the parking lot, until he reached the safety of the store.

Mrs. Fremont was just starting down the last row. "It took you a long time," she scolded.

"I thought I was going to have to come find you and my coupons."

"Sorry," Marvin mumbled. He moved his face as close to his mother's as he could. "Mom," he said in an urgent whisper. "Mr. Wolfe and another man were in the parking lot plotting a murder. Really," he added when he saw his mother's expression. "I heard them."

"Oh, Marvin." Mrs. Fremont shook her head. "You have got to stop reading those awful comics."

"But I—"

"I'll be ready to check out in a few minutes," Mrs. Fremont interrupted briskly. "Go get Sarah and catch up with me. You can tell me all about it when we get home." She started down the aisle before Marvin could explain further.

Sarah was still reading the same magazine. "I just heard two men plotting a murder," Marvin burst out when he saw her.

Sarah stared at him. Then a slow smile crossed her face. "That was handy—hearing about a murder two minutes after you decided to become a detective," she said with a chuckle.

Just then Mr. Wolfe entered the store. Marvin peered at him over the revolving rack. "It's not a joke," he hissed. A pretty young woman with soft blond hair walked by, blocking Marvin's view of Mr. Wolfe. Marvin stretched on his toes, trying to see past her, but suddenly his foot slipped, and he lost his balance. He grabbed for the rack of comic books to steady himself, but it swayed and tipped toward the aisle. Marvin tried desperately to stop his fall, but the base of the rack slid forward, and over they both went with a noisy and terrifying crash.

THREE

Howls
IN THE
NIGHT

Before the rack hit the floor, Mr. Wolfe was in motion. First he gallantly pushed the blond woman out of the way, then he rushed to Marvin. He brushed aside the comic books and asked, "Are you all right? That was quite a fall."

Rubbing a bruised knee, Marvin peered up at his neighbor. Mr. Wolfe had a curly red beard. When he smiled, Marvin could see his bright white teeth. It was amazing how much he looked like the werewolf in the comic. Right now Mr. Wolfe was pretending to be nice and concerned, but Marvin was not fooled by his friendly smile.

In all the books he'd read, criminals often had strange conversations like the one he'd just overheard. Most of these conversations took place in dark alleys or cemeteries or other creepy places. A grocery store parking lot did not seem to be a good place to plot a murder. But Mr. Wolfe's friend had been in a hurry. Perhaps he thought no one would pay any attention. Whatever the reason, he'd made a big mistake. Someone named Henry was in terrible danger. Marvin was determined to find him and warn him before it was too late.

A large crowd of Saturday shoppers had already gathered by the fallen magazine rack. "Better not move," said a soft voice. It was the blond woman. "You might be injured."

Assuring her he was all right, Marvin ignored Mr. Wolfe's hand and stood up. By now Mr. McNaulty had come running over. He did not look very happy. He ordered the box boys to straighten the mess. Marvin saw that Sarah had disappeared, but a second later he understood why. She returned dragging her mother by the hand. In her other hand, Mrs. Fremont was still holding a can of peas.

Marvin knew his mother was mentally checking for injuries, but, finding none, a slow red flush crept up her neck.

"How could you knock over a whole rack like that?" Mrs. Fremont asked crossly.

"I was trying to watch Mr. Wolfe," Marvin hissed, glancing quickly at his neighbor, who was talking to the pretty blond woman.

Satisfied that he was not listening, Marvin continued. "I told you he was in the parking lot, plotting a murder."

"Marvin, you have got to stop letting your imagination get out of hand," Mrs. Fremont scolded.

"I don't," Marvin protested.

Sarah laughed. "How about when you read that book about UFOs? The next night you thought you saw one hovering above our house."

"I admit I thought that weather balloon was a UFO," Marvin said. "But this is different. I know what I heard."

It was plain from the look on Mrs. Fremont's face that she did not believe him. Marvin gave up and helped replace the comic books in the rack.

Five minutes later the shoppers had returned to going about their business. Mr. McNaulty and Marvin's mother had taken turns apologizing to each other, and Mr. Wolfe had left the store with the pretty woman.

Mrs. Fremont looked grim as she paid for the groceries. "Now, young man," she said as she drove back to the house, "no more spying on neighbors."

"Maybe you just misunderstood what you

heard," Sarah offered. "Maybe Henry's a dog and Mr. Fiumera is allergic to him. They might get rid of Henry by finding him a new home."

"The man said *eliminate* . . . ," Marvin began.

"Now listen," his mother interrupted. "Mr. Wolfe doesn't socialize much, and it does seem odd for a single man to want such a large house. But he seems very nice. I don't want you to bother him. Understood?"

Marvin nodded, but all evening he worried about the conversation. When he went to bed, he tossed and turned until his sheets were wrapped in uncomfortable knots. Finally he fell asleep. In his dreams he was Henry. He seemed to be running down a dark alley. Behind him he could hear heavy footsteps, but he was too afraid to turn around to see who was there. At last he gathered his courage for a quick peek. It was Mr. Wolfe! He was smiling, showing his large white teeth. To Marvin's horror, the teeth were becoming sharp and pointed, and Mr. Wolfe's face seemed to be growing alarmingly hairy. Marvin awoke with a jump. "Werewolf," he whispered. He clicked on his light and sat on the edge of the bed until his heart stopped pounding.

At last he straightened his shoulders. No matter what anyone said, he was going to solve this mystery. He padded over to his desk and searched until he found a small lined notebook. He wrote down the conversation in the parking lot exactly as he remembered it. After that he jotted: *1. Who is Henry? 2. Why does Mr. Wolfe have to get rid of him?*

All that thinking was making him thirsty. Taking the notebook with him, he padded to the kitchen in his bare feet for a drink of milk. Mr. and Mrs. Fremont had gone to bed, and the house was silent. Even the usually warm, cozy kitchen seemed creepy. Although he tried to ignore it, the darkness through the dining room door made him uneasy. Marvin drank his milk quickly and ate two cookies. Then he snapped off the light and paused by the kitchen window before going back to bed. The full moon was partly covered by clouds, but it was still bright enough to see.

Mr. Wolfe's upstairs lights were off, but a faint light from the basement window cast a shadowy glow on the overgrown shrubbery in the yard. Now and then the light flickered, as though someone was walking in front of it. I wonder why Mr. Wolfe is in his basement at two o'clock in the morning, Marvin thought.

There was a stealthy creak in the floor behind him. Marvin froze. What if Mr. Wolfe was not in his basement? What if right this very minute he was creeping up behind him? The floor creaked again. Marvin stayed very still, not even daring to take a breath. Someone was definitely moving softly through the house, heading straight for the kitchen!

Suddenly the light flicked on. "What are you doing standing in the dark in the middle of the night?" asked Sarah.

Marvin let out the breath he'd been holding and sat down quickly so that Sarah could not see how much his knees were shaking. "Why are you sneaking around the house in the middle of the night?" he snapped.

Sarah grinned at Marvin's pale face. "Scared you, didn't I? But I wasn't sneaking around. I was walking quietly so I wouldn't wake up Mom and Dad. You woke me up when you went downstairs."

"I was looking at Mr. Wolfe's house," Marvin confessed.

Sarah poured herself a glass of milk and added two heaping teaspoons of chocolate. She took a big gulp, leaving a chocolate mustache over her lip. Then she cupped her hands against the window and looked out. "It is the creepiest house I've ever seen."

Marvin nodded. Sarah was right. The house

was creepy. It was the oldest house in the neighborhood. For years it had been empty and
neglected. Some of the windows had been broken, the door sagged, and ragged bushes nearly
covered the front steps. Then suddenly Mr.
Wolfe had moved in.

He had improved the house, replacing the
broken windows and fixing the sagging front
door. But even with a new coat of paint the
house still looked spooky.

"We'd better go back to bed before we wake
up Mom and Dad," Sarah said. "You might as
well forget about solving any mysteries. There
is probably a perfectly logical explanation for
the conversation you heard. And anyway, who
is this Henry? I've never seen anyone at Mr.
Wolfe's house except carpenters and painters."

Marvin pointed to the beam of light from the
window. "Maybe he keeps Henry a prisoner in
the basement."

Sarah laughed nervously. "Don't be silly.
Why would he do that?"

Marvin did not get a chance to answer.
Before he could speak, they heard a strange
sound. It was a low, mournful sound, a terrible
howling noise that made the hair stand up on
the back of their necks. *"Ahooo, Ahoooo."*

"Did you hear that?" Sarah whispered.

"It sounded like . . . a wolf!" Marvin said in a shaky voice. He shivered. "I know we're not supposed to believe in monsters and all that, but did you ever wonder about it? What if there really are monsters, and people just don't tell their kids because they don't want to scare them?"

"I don't believe in monsters," Sarah said, sounding as though she was trying to convince herself. "But if I did, I imagine they would sound just like that."

Marvin nodded slowly. "Full moon, creepy house, howling. It's no wonder Mr. Wolfe is talking about eliminating someone. I think Mr. Wolfe really is a wolf—a werewolf!"

FOUR

Some
DETECTIVE
WORK

The next afternoon Marvin sat on his front porch steps, eating a bologna sandwich and watching Mr. Wolfe's house. It was a bright, warm day, the kind that happens after the first October frost. The trees were a blaze of red and gold, and just enough leaves had fallen to make a crunchy sound underfoot. Marvin hoped the warm weather would last through Halloween. It was much more fun to go trick-or-treating when costumes didn't have to be hidden under heavy coats.

Marvin had tucked his notebook into his pants pocket, but so far nothing had happened worth writing down. He was hoping to catch a glimpse of someone who might be Henry. Perhaps he was the owner of the blue sports car parked in Mr. Wolfe's driveway.

Sarah came outside carrying her skates. Her

camera swung from a cord around her neck. She sat on the step beside Marvin while she laced up her skates. "Want to come skating with me?" she coaxed.

"I'm watching to see if that blue car belongs to Henry," Marvin said.

"Jeepers, Marvin. After that noise we heard last night, I don't even want to think about Mr. Wolfe."

Marvin shook his head. "I just feel I have to find out who Henry is and warn him."

A delivery van pulled up behind the sports car, and the driver went to the door, carrying a small brown box. Marvin watched with interest as Mr. Wolfe signed for the package. He went inside, leaving the door ajar. Just then a small brown-and-white-spotted dog pushed through the crack. He bounded down the front steps and then trotted over to Marvin and Sarah. The dog's tail waved in friendly circles.

"Mr. Wolfe has a dog," Sarah said. She scratched the dog's ears, making his tail spin even faster. "Was that you making all that noise last night?" she crooned.

"Do you really think a little dog like that could make the noise we heard?" Marvin asked. He'd be a little disappointed if the mystery was so easily solved.

The dog eyed Marvin's sandwich hopefully, until Marvin broke off a bite and handed it to him. The little dog gulped it down without chewing and begged with his eyes for more.

"I'll bet his name is Henry," Sarah said briskly. "And I'll bet that awful howling is why Mr. Wolfe has to get rid of him."

Marvin wasn't convinced. "Then how come we've never heard him before? And why would Mr. Fiumera care about how much time Mr. Wolfe is spending with his dog?"

Sarah and Marvin were glum, both remembering the terrible howling. Who would take a dog that made a noise like that? Mr. Wolfe looked out the door.

"Here, Jack," Mr. Wolfe called from his front porch. The little dog stood up, but he still looked longingly at the last bite of sandwich.

Mr. Wolfe had not seen Jack with the twins. "Here, Jack," he called again, sounding worried.

"I guess now we know for sure that Henry isn't a dog," Sarah said quietly. She stood up and waved to Mr. Wolfe. "He's over here."

Marvin gave Jack the last piece of sandwich. Jack gulped it down and trotted back home, his tail flying happily.

"Thanks." Mr. Wolfe bent down and patted his dog. "Jack's been staying with friends while

I got the house in order. He's been here for only a few days. I was afraid he would run off and get lost. Say," he added as he stood up, "I hope Jack didn't keep you awake last night. I tried tying him outside, but he didn't like it."

Sarah skated in circles along the front walk and watched Jack follow Mr. Wolfe back to the house. "He's nice to his dog...." Her voice trailed off uncertainly. "You must have misunderstood the conversation. Mr. Wolfe wouldn't hurt anybody."

"I heard every word, just like I told you," Marvin said grimly. He thought about his dream the night before.

Mr. Fremont stepped outside carrying the hedge trimmers. Marvin listened to the steady buzz as his father went to work on a large bush in the front yard.

Mr. Wolfe came back outside with a plastic recycling bag and put it in his garage. "Nice day," he called over cheerfully when Mr. Fremont switched off the hedge trimmers.

"Yes, it is," Mr. Fremont answered. "I want to tell you that the whole neighborhood appreciates how you're cleaning up your property."

"Thanks," said Mr. Wolfe. "Would you like to see what I'm doing inside?"

Mr. Fremont left the hedge trimmers by the

bushes and walked across the yard. "Can we see, too?" Marvin asked quickly.

"Sure," Mr. Wolfe said with a smile.

Marvin waited impatiently while Sarah quickly pulled off her skates and jammed her feet back into her shoes. Then they ran to catch up with Mr. Wolfe and their father. All the curtains in Mr. Wolfe's house were pulled shut, and even in the bright sunlight it looked dark and ominous. Marvin shivered. "I'm sure not going to go trick-or-treating here on Halloween," he whispered. "I don't care how much he redecorated it."

"Fixing up old houses is a hobby of mine," Mr. Wolfe was telling Mr. Fremont. "The inside of the house was really a mess when I bought it. Everything was dirty and covered with cobwebs. But underneath it all, I knew there was a good solid house."

Marvin shuddered at the mention of cobwebs, furtively checking the corners of the ceiling. But inside, the house was surprisingly nice. It smelled of fresh paint and polish.

Mr. Wolfe led the way to the kitchen. To Marvin's surprise, the blond woman he had seen at the grocery store was sitting at the kitchen table, drinking a cup of coffee.

"This is Miss Graves," Mr. Wolfe told them.

Miss Graves had an open, pretty smile. "Hello," she said. Then her eyes widened. "You're the boy who knocked over the rack at McNaulty's."

"Sorry," Marvin mumbled, his face red.

Miss Graves continued to smile. "Don't apologize. If you hadn't knocked over that rack, Mr. Wolfe and I might never have met."

"Miss Graves just moved to Liberty Corners, too. She teaches archaeology at the college," Mr. Wolfe told Mr. Fremont. "We started talking at the grocery store yesterday, and I discovered that she likes old houses. So I invited her over to see what I was doing."

Liberty Corners boasted a small private college that was one of the best in Ohio. Marvin looked at Miss Graves with interest. With her blond hair swept back and held with a large barrette, she looked more like a student than a college professor.

Leaving Miss Graves to finish her coffee, Marvin and Sarah followed their father as Mr. Wolfe took them on a tour of the house. Jack padded quietly after them.

Mr. Wolfe pointed to one door. "This goes to the attic. When I moved in, it was infested with bats."

"Bats!" Sarah squeaked.

"Oh, I don't really mind," said Mr. Wolfe with a toothy grin. "Bats are really rather nice creatures to have around. Most people don't realize how many bugs they eat every night."

Mr. Wolfe continued his tour of the house. Marvin tried not to think about the attic's occupants, concentrating instead on collecting clues. One of the bedrooms was empty, but it had been freshly painted a soft yellow. Unseen by Mr. Wolfe, Marvin sneaked in and peeked in the closet. "Empty," he whispered.

The next room was Mr. Wolfe's. "Haven't had a chance to do anything in here yet," he apologized. It was a large room paneled in a dark brown wood. Three long grooves were cut into the wall beside the door. Mr. Wolfe noticed Marvin examining the scratches. "The furniture movers scratched it when they brought in that mirror," he said. "I think I can cover them with some wood stain."

Marvin gave Sarah a meaningful glance as Mr. Wolfe looked away. "Looks like claw marks to me," he whispered.

The brown box the delivery man had given Mr. Wolfe was sitting on the dresser. Marvin saw Sarah lean over and read the label.

"Was it anything interesting?" Marvin asked

quietly as they peeked in a third bedroom.

Sarah shrugged. "Not really. It was from a computer-parts company."

They hurried to catch up with Mr. Wolfe and their father. "I'll bet your friend Henry likes the way you fixed up the house," Marvin said.

Mr. Wolfe's eyes narrowed. "Who?"

"Doesn't someone else live here?" asked Sarah.

Mr. Wolfe did not look as friendly as he had a minute before. "I live alone," he said. His voice was cold.

"I guess we were mixed up," Marvin explained awkwardly. "I thought someone else lived here, too."

There was an uncomfortable silence as Mr. Wolfe stared at them. Mr. Fremont had gone into the bathroom and was studying the carved moldings around the ceiling. He patted the old claw-footed tub. "They don't make big tubs like this anymore," he said admiringly. He and Mr. Wolfe discussed boring things like plaster and wall studs as they walked through the rest of the house. Mr. Wolfe occasionally looked over at Sarah and Marvin with a puzzled expression.

At last they returned to the kitchen. Miss Graves was thumbing through a huge book of wallpaper samples. "Isn't it a wonderful old house?" she asked.

Marvin noticed a door at one end of the kitchen. "Is this a closet?" he asked, reaching for the handle.

Mr. Wolfe looked alarmed. He stepped over quickly and firmly held the door closed. "That's just the basement. You wouldn't want to go down there. It's a mess, and the stairs are not very safe. I haven't done anything down there yet."

The twins exchanged a look. If it was so dangerous and still such a mess, what was he doing down there so late last night?

"We'd better be going," said Mr. Fremont.

Marvin gave one longing glance at the basement door. They had toured the entire house without the slightest clue about Henry, except for Mr. Wolfe's obvious discomfort that they knew his name. Whoever Henry was, Marvin was sure the answer was behind that forbidden door.

FIVE

Another
STRANGE
CONVERSATION

After they said good-bye to Mr. Wolfe, Mr. Fremont went back to work trimming the shrubs and Sarah laced up her skates and rolled away. Marvin sat back down on the porch steps, jotting ideas in his notebook. For a few minutes he considered telling his father about his suspicions, but then he decided against it. It had been obvious that his father and Mr. Wolfe had struck up a friendship. Probably because of their mutual interest in wall studs, Marvin thought with a sigh. After a while Miss Graves came out of the house. She waved at Marvin as she backed the blue car out of the drive. Marvin stared thoughtfully after her. From Marvin's backyard came the sound of the hedge trimmers, but Mr. Wolfe's house remained quiet. Marvin was tempted to put on his skates and find Sarah. After all, even if Mr. Wolfe was some sort of monster, what could he do about it? He could not even handle Mean Ernie. And what about Miss Graves and his dad? They seemed to think Mr. Wolfe was all right. On the other hand, if Mr. Wolfe was some kind of monster, then Miss Graves and his father might be in danger.

Sarah glided up to the steps. "Are you going to sit there all day? Come on, skate with me."

Marvin shut his notebook and reluctantly went to get his skates. He was not a very good skater. Sarah skimmed along gracefully, turning circles and skating backward when Marvin fell behind. They skated around the block and stopped in front of their own house.

"Hey, there's Mr. Wolfe," Sarah said. "I wonder where he's going in such a hurry."

Mr. Wolfe was walking briskly in the direction of the highway and Liberty Corners's small business district.

"Let's follow him," Marvin said.

"Maybe we should check out his house while he's gone," Sarah said. "We could peek in that basement window. If we spot any evidence, I could take a picture," she offered, patting the camera around her neck.

Marvin started to agree. Then he remembered that their father was still working in the yard.

"We'll do that later. Maybe he's going to find Henry right now. It can't be very far or he would have taken his car." He hesitated. "Let's take off our skates. It will be a lot easier to stay out of sight without them."

They quickly removed the skates and slipped on their shoes. "Hurry," Marvin urged. "We're going to lose him." He stuffed the notebook in his back pocket and hurried after Mr. Wolfe, darting behind bushes now and then to stay hidden, in case Mr. Wolfe looked back.

Mr. Wolfe strode purposefully, unaware that he was being followed. Marvin and Sarah kept at a safe distance.

Suddenly Mr. Wolfe stopped by the entrance into an alley. "Where's he going now?" Sarah whispered.

Mr. Wolfe looked around furtively before he started down the alley. The twins had just barely enough time to dive behind some shrubs so they wouldn't be noticed.

"Do you think he saw us?" Marvin whispered.

"I don't think so," Sarah said.

Keeping hidden, they peeked down the alley.

Marvin snapped his fingers. "I know where he's going. Frankie's garage is here."

A highway ran through this part of Liberty Corners. Across the highway was the small shopping center where Mrs. Fremont bought her groceries. On this side there were several small businesses and restaurants. Squeezed in behind a pizza shop, Frankie had a run-down garage, where he sometimes repaired cars. The big overhead doors opened into the short alley that ran along behind. The other side of the alley was lined with a thick row of trees and shrubs, separating the residential area and giving Marvin and Sarah good cover.

Frankie stepped out of the garage and closed the doors too quickly for Marvin to be able to see inside. He noticed that Frankie had a streak of yellow paint across his cheek. Mr. Wolfe started talking, but Marvin was too far away to hear. Marvin was burning with curiosity. "What do you suppose Mr. Wolfe is doing with Frankie?" he asked Sarah in a whisper. Marvin always tried to avoid running into the handy-man. Once when Marvin had fallen off his bike and skinned himself quite badly, he had looked up and seen Frankie watching across the street. Instead of running to help like most grown-ups would, Frankie had only snickered and turned back to his work.

"Maybe he just needs him to do some work on his house," Sarah suggested.

"Come on," Marvin encouraged Sarah. "Let's get closer so we can hear what they're saying."

"Wait a second," Sarah whispered. She aimed her camera at the two men and quickly snapped a picture.

"Good thinking," Marvin whispered. Thick patches of ragweed and straggly bushes gave them good cover as they inched along until they were close enough to hear.

"Heavy," Mr. Wolfe was saying. "About a hundred and fifty pounds deadweight."

"Don't worry about that," Frankie said. "I'm strong."

"Good. Then pick it up about ten o'clock tomorrow night." Mr. Wolfe hesitated. "And of course you understand that you can't discuss this with anyone."

"You can depend on me," Frankie said solemnly. Mr. Wolfe cut through the pizza restaurant's parking lot, heading for the highway, and Frankie stared after him.

Marvin's nose twitched from the ragweed. His heart was pounding so loudly, he was sure

Frankie would hear. He rubbed at his nose, but before he could stop himself, a loud sneeze exploded from him. *Ka-chew*.

Frankie whirled around and spotted them immediately. "Hey," he growled. "What are you two doing snooping around?" His cold black eyes narrowed suspiciously.

"We were just walking to the store," Sarah said, straightening up. "This is a public alley."

Marvin gave Sarah an admiring glance.

"Then get going. And quit sneaking around like little spies."

Marvin looked after Mr. Wolfe, hoping the bearded man hadn't realized that he and Frankie had been overheard. But he had not turned around. He was waiting for the traffic to clear so he could cross the highway. Trying to look innocent, Marvin and Sarah hurried to catch up.

SIX

Monster SHOPPING

Liberty Corners Shopping Center was a small cluster of shops with a medium-size discount store on one end. Mrs. Fremont sometimes purchased a dress at Madame Victoria's. Marvin was pleased to see that Madame Victoria's was not Mr. Wolfe's destination. Marvin had already put Madame Victoria's on the top of his worst-places-to-go list, just above McNaulty's grocery store and the beauty parlor.

Mr. Wolfe passed Madame Victoria's and the small gift shop next to it.

"He's going to the discount store," Sarah said just as Mr. Wolfe disappeared through the door of the store.

They hung back a minute before they followed him. Mr. Wolfe was in the men's department, looking at a pair of black pants. "Jeepers.

37

That's not very exciting," Sarah said. "He's just buying himself some clothes."

"He is buying clothes, but not for himself," Marvin said.

"How do you know that?" Sarah asked.

"Mr. Wolfe must be at least six feet tall. But look at those pants he's holding up. They are way too short for him," Marvin pointed out.

"Then why is he buying them?" Sarah asked. An answer occurred to them both at the same time. "For Henry," they said together.

Marvin stayed two rows away. He tried on several baseball hats, pretending to be shopping, but all the while he kept Mr. Wolfe in sight. Mr. Wolfe draped the pants over his arm and began looking at white shirts.

Marvin tried on an Ohio Buckeyes hat, admiring himself in the mirror. In the meantime, Sarah had walked over to the jewelry counter. She held up a pair of earrings. "I wish Mom and Dad would let me pierce my ears," she said.

Marvin suddenly realized that Mr. Wolfe was no longer in sight. "Quick." He motioned to his sister. "You go down that row."

Sarah scurried off in one direction and Marvin in another. He gave a sigh of relief. Mr. Wolfe was still shopping. Now he seemed to be looking at ladies' coats. Marvin leaned across a counter to see better, when suddenly he realized something horrible. He was right in the middle of the ladies' underwear department. The counter he was leaning on was stacked high with lacy silk underpants.

"May I help you?" asked an unfriendly voice.

Marvin looked up at the clerk's disapproving stare. The clerk was very tall, and her skinny eyebrows were scrunched into a frown.

"I was just looking," Marvin said without thinking. Then as the clerk's frown deepened, he realized what he'd said. "For a present," he amended quickly. "For my mother."

The skinny eyebrows smoothed down, and the clerk almost managed a smile. "Perhaps your mother would be happier with a necklace or a pretty vase."

Marvin blushed furiously. "That's a good idea." He circled quickly around the underwear counter and ran right into Mr. Wolfe.

"Hello, neighbor," Mr. Wolfe said heartily. "Doing some shopping?"

"I—I'm looking for something for my mother's birthday," Marvin said, desperately repeating his story.

"Maybe she'd like a nice black cape like this." Mr. Wolfe twirled the black cape he was holding,

so that Marvin could admire it. Then he leaned over, and in a spooky, quiet voice he whispered, "It is almost Halloween, after all."

"Er, I don't think so," Marvin said. "I don't think she likes black all that much."

Mr. Wolfe smiled, showing his unusually bright white teeth. "I'm buying this for a friend. He loves black."

A tiny shiver ran down Marvin's spine as he looked at the clothes Mr. Wolfe was buying: black pants, white ruffled shirt, black cape. Mr. Wolfe wasn't buying clothes for Henry. Marvin knew exactly who wore clothes like that— Dracula!

SEVEN

The Murderer NEXT DOOR

On Monday morning Sarah waved good-bye at the school entrance and went off to her classroom. Elated that he'd made it this far without running into Mean Ernie, Marvin headed for his own class. But Marvin turned a corner and there he was—Mean Ernie—leaning against the wall with his arms crossed.

"Hey, four-eyes," he shouted. "I saw you in the grocery store Saturday. You weren't avoiding me by any chance, were you?"

Marvin looked at the larger boy and forced himself to smile. "Were you there?" he said in a voice he hoped sounded innocent. "I didn't see you."

Ernie gave him a suspicious look. He shoved Marvin roughly back against the wall with the tips of his fingers. "Good," he sneered. "I'd hate to think you were ignoring me, especially when we're such good friends."

Marvin was saved by the morning bell. Both boys slid into their seats at the last minute.

An encounter with Ernie usually left Marvin miserable all day. But today his mind was so full of the mystery, there was room for little else. He spent most of the afternoon organizing his notebook. On one sheet he wrote all his suspicions. On another he wrote all the clues. Twice, Mrs. Pfeiffer had to scold him for not paying attention.

Marvin didn't get a chance to show the notebook to Sarah until that evening. They were up in Sarah's darkened bedroom, which faced Mr. Wolfe's house. For an hour they had been watching out the window, taking turns with Mr. Fremont's old binoculars. According to the conversation they'd overheard, Frankie would show up around ten.

"Jeepers!" Sarah said after she read Marvin's notes. "I can't figure out what is going on. First you think somebody named Henry is being murdered. Then you suspect Mr. Wolfe is really a werewolf. Now it seems as though he's friends with Dracula. Do you think it could all be some weird kind of joke?"

"You heard Mr. Wolfe say how much he liked bats. And I told you about the Dracula clothes he was buying," Marvin reminded her. "And the conversation with Frankie—did that sound like a joke?"

Sarah shook her head.

"And that night we heard the howling, there was a full moon," Marvin added. "I haven't heard Jack howl any other night."

Although the room was dark, there was enough moonlight for Marvin to write by. He put down in his notebook: *9:45. Suspect still inside house.*

So far nothing mysterious had happened. The only signs of life were Jack, who was asleep on the front porch, and a faint light coming from Mr. Wolfe's basement window.

"I'm getting sleepy," Sarah said with a yawn.

"Something's bound to happen anytime now," Marvin assured her. "He told Frankie to come at ten o'clock."

"Well, this is boring," Sarah said crossly.

"A good detective is always patient," Marvin told her.

He glanced out of the window again and yawned himself. It was hard to stay awake in the dark. Usually he grumbled when his parents sent him to bed. Tonight they had given him an odd look when he had gone upstairs without complaining. The Fremonts encouraged their children to develop their own hobbies and interests, but Marvin knew these would not include spying on the neighbor's house instead of sleeping.

He glanced at Mr. Wolfe's house again. Even though it was almost ten, everything was still quiet.

A dark shadow swooped in front of the window. Marvin gasped and nearly dropped the binoculars.

"What was it?" Sarah whispered.

"I think it was a bat," Marvin said.

"Maybe it's just eating bugs like Mr. Wolfe said," Sarah said hopefully.

"And maybe it wants to drink your blood," Marvin said in a spooky voice.

"Stop that," Sarah said crossly. "Oh, there's another one." She groaned as a second shadow swept by.

Marvin shivered. They sat in silence for five more minutes before Sarah stood up and stretched.

"If we solve this case, we'll be famous," Marvin coaxed. He took off his glasses and cleaned them on his shirt. "We might even get our pictures in the paper. Maybe Mean Ernie will see it and stop calling me a runt."

Sarah gave Marvin an understanding glance. She pirouetted across the room and did a karate chop in the air. "Why don't you let me talk to him?"

"Don't you dare," Marvin said sharply. "Everyone in school would say I had my sister protect me. I'd never live it down. And besides, just because you had a few karate lessons doesn't mean you're tougher than Mean Ernie."

Sarah leapt across the floor again, but Marvin jumped up and grabbed her arm.

"You sound like a herd of elephants," he hissed. "Do you want Mom and Dad to hear?"

Sarah made a face. "My teacher says I am very graceful."

Marvin choked back a laugh. It was Sarah's room, after all. She was letting him watch from her window, even though he was not usually allowed in.

"I guess you are getting pretty good," he said grudgingly. "But Mom and Dad still might hear you." Marvin yawned and glanced out the window. "Uh oh," he whispered. "I think Frankie's here."

An old pickup truck stopped in the driveway next door. While Marvin had been talking to Sarah, the basement light had gone out in Mr. Wolfe's house. The front door opened, and Mr. Wolfe emerged just as the handyman jumped out of his truck. They spoke a few words. Then Frankie walked around and opened the door on the passenger side while Mr. Wolfe walked back in the house.

"It's a good thing the moon is so bright," Marvin said. "We can see everything."

Mr. Wolfe came back out of the house, carrying something over his shoulder. Even though it was covered with a sheet, that something looked dreadfully like a body.

"Oh, jeepers. You were right," Sarah whispered, looking stricken. "There really *was* a Henry. And Mr. Wolfe has already murdered him."

With a sickening lurch in his stomach, Marvin watched as Mr. Wolfe settled the bundle in the passenger side of Frankie's old pickup truck. Suddenly Mr. Wolfe stared at the Fremont house, and for the fraction of a second before Marvin ducked behind the curtain, their eyes seemed to meet. When he finally peeked out again, Mr. Wolfe was walking back inside his

house. Then as Marvin and Sarah watched in speechless horror, Frankie climbed into the driver's seat and backed the truck quickly into the street.

Poor HENRY

Marvin finally found his voice. "Did you see that?"

Sarah shook her head. "I can't believe it. I really thought he seemed kind of nice. I didn't really believe all that stuff about him being a murderer," she confessed. "Sorry."

"That's okay. I guess it does sound pretty wild. Who would ever think something so terrible could happen in a little town like Liberty Corners?"

Marvin glanced out the window. All the lights were out. "I guess he's gone to bed," he said.

He was silent for a minute. "In this comic book I read, the guy was just an ordinary person most of the time. He couldn't stop himself from turning into a werewolf and killing people," he said finally.

Sarah hit her head with her fist. "My camera! It happened so fast, I forgot to take a picture."

"It's a good thing. Mr. Wolfe would have seen the flash. I'm afraid he might have seen us anyway."

"If I'm ever going to be a famous photographer, I have to be ready to snap a picture wherever the action is. And now I had a chance to take a picture of a murderer and I forgot," Sarah said, groaning.

"Forget about the camera," Marvin said. "What are we going to do? I thought I could find out who Henry was and warn him. Now it's too late."

"We should have told Mom and Dad," Sarah said.

Marvin nodded. "I tried to, remember? Mom didn't believe me."

"Well, we have to tell them now," Sarah said.

"They still wouldn't believe it," Marvin said thoughtfully. "They'd just say we had overactive imaginations. And then we'd be in trouble for snooping. I wish I hadn't mentioned Henry to Mr. Wolfe. I'm sure he suspects we've been watching. If Mom and Dad accidentally said something to Mr. Wolfe, he'd know for sure. He might even try to get rid of us."

Sarah looked pale. "How about the police? They'd know what to do."

Marvin shook his head. "Same thing. They'd never believe a couple of kids. We have to get some evidence first."

"How can we do that?" Sarah asked with a worried glance out the window.

"Did you notice how easily Mr. Wolfe carried the body? He must be awfully strong." Marvin scribbled something in his notebook. "Maybe Henry was a prisoner in that basement room all this time. We need to get inside the house and look for evidence—like bloodstains on the floor. Then we'd have proof that Mr. Wolfe killed Henry."

"Did I hear you say *we*?" Sarah asked. "I'm not going near that house—and neither will you, if you have any brains."

"Can you sleep knowing there is a murderer next door? Remember, your bedroom windows are on this side of the house."

Sarah pulled her curtains together tightly. "Where do you suppose Frankie took the body?" she asked.

Marvin snapped his fingers. "That's it. Somebody's bound to find the body. We'll just wait until they do. Then we'll report what we saw. The police will have to believe us when they have a body for evidence."

"All right," Sarah agreed. "That's safer than trying to get inside Mr. Wolfe's house. But until the body is found, we won't say a word to anyone. And if we see Mr. Wolfe, we'll have to act real friendly, like we don't suspect anything."

Marvin crept quietly across the hall to his own room and climbed into bed, but he was too excited and nervous to fall asleep. When his parents came in to check, as they did every night, Marvin made his breathing even and kept his eyes closed. His mother pulled up the covers and tucked them in. Usually Marvin thought he was too old to have his mother tuck him in every night. But somehow tonight, he was very glad she did.

NINE

A Sinister INVITATION

Liberty Corners was a quiet town. The discovery of a body would be big news. Yet two days went by without a word. Mr. Wolfe did not act like a man with dark secrets to hide. When the twins got home from school, his house repairs were going on as usual. Every evening, though, the light flicked on in the basement room, and Sarah reported that it remained on until long after they went to bed. They began to grow impatient.

Mr. Wolfe had told Mrs. Fremont that until his kitchen was done he liked to eat out. Marvin noticed that he often left the house around six. So on Wednesday evening, the twins sneaked out after dinner, hoping to get a peek into Mr. Wolfe's basement window before he returned.

Suddenly, from inside the house Jack began to bark. Marvin and Sarah feared that their parents would hear and look out the window. They fled back to their yard just before the front door opened. Mr. Wolfe was home! The next day the window was securely covered with a curtain, as though Mr. Wolfe had known they'd been there.

Every day Marvin waited eagerly for the paperboy to bring the evening paper so he could read the headlines before anyone else. On Thursday the only item of interest was that Mrs. Hanson's car had been stolen.

"Poor Mrs. Hanson," said Mrs. Fremont. "She was so proud of her car. I hope the police find it."

Marvin was more interested in missing bodies. Even Sarah looked worried. "What if Frankie buried it?" she asked when they were alone.

Marvin nodded glumly. "We'll just have to hope someone finds it anyway."

In the meantime it was hard to remain quiet at school. The next afternoon when Mean Ernie blocked the sidewalk on the way home from school, Marvin wanted to tell him that a person who has witnessed a murder is not going to be afraid of a fourth-grade bully. But at the last second he thought better of it and ducked away across Mrs. Parson's backyard.

"I've never seen you take such an interest in the paper," Mrs. Fremont remarked later that evening. She looked pleased. Marvin wondered what she would think if she knew the real reason. He shook his head at Sarah to let her know there was still no mention of a body having been found.

"Mrs. Pfeiffer wants us to keep up on current events for social studies," Marvin explained feebly.

"Well, I think it's wonderful that your teacher encourages her students to read the news. But it's such a lovely evening. Why don't you two scoot outside while I cook dinner. We won't have many more warm days like this."

Mrs. Fremont looked at the calendar. "My goodness. Halloween is only a week away. We had better decide about your costumes." She reached into the refrigerator for lettuce and tomatoes to make a salad.

"What do you want to do?" Sarah asked as they buttoned their jackets.

"We could shoot a few baskets," Marvin suggested. "That way, we can watch Mr. Wolfe's house."

Miss Graves's small blue car was parked in Mr. Wolfe's driveway. "I see Mr. Wolfe has company. I hope she gets out of there alive," Sarah said. She went to the garage and got the ball. With nervous glances over her shoulder at Mr.

Wolfe's house, she threw it at the hoop Mr. Fremont had attached to the garage. Marvin grabbed the ball and sank a perfect shot. For a few minutes they concentrated on the game, forgetting about the house next door. Marvin had to put every ounce of energy into beating Sarah. When she tried, she was really a better player than Marvin, and when she did win, she never let him forget it.

Suddenly, just as he was ready to shoot, Sarah knocked the ball out of his hands and sent it spinning across their own driveway and into Mr. Wolfe's. It rolled to a stop behind Miss Graves's car. They both started to run after it, but before they could retrieve it, Miss Graves neatly scooped it up and lobbed in a perfect basket. Neither Marvin nor Sarah had noticed her come outside.

"Hi, Miss Graves," Marvin said.

"Call me Charlotte," she said. "I hope I didn't spoil your game. I haven't had a chance to play basketball for a long time."

Smiling shyly, Marvin picked up the ball and passed it to her. Charlotte Graves neatly made a second basket. "I haven't lost my touch," she exclaimed happily.

She made three more baskets in a row. "You're really good," Sarah said admiringly as she threw her the ball to try again.

Marvin remembered that Mr. Wolfe had told them Miss Graves taught archaeology at the college. "Being an archaeologist sounds really interesting," he said. "We're studying about mound builders in school."

"I'd love to go to Egypt someday and do some research on them," Miss Graves answered.

Marvin gave Sarah a look. Miss Graves was not a very good archaeologist if she didn't even know about the mound builders. In school they had studied the Hopewell culture. Mrs. Pfeiffer had explained that they were a group of prehistoric Native Americans who had left mysterious mounds scattered throughout the Midwest. Nobody is sure exactly why the mounds were built, although some scientists believe they were intended to be tombs.

Mr. Wolfe came out the back door, followed by Jack. The little dog trotted to them, and Marvin bent to scratch his ears.

"What's going on?" Mr. Wolfe asked. His voice sounded friendly.

Charlotte Graves tossed Mr. Wolfe the ball. "I was just shooting a few baskets with your neighbors. Here, you try one."

Marvin and Sarah exchanged an anxious

glance. Playing basketball with a werewolf was not a fun idea. But Mr. Wolfe took the ball and calmly threw it from where he stood. It ringed the hoop for a split second before dropping through.

"Not bad, if I do say so myself," Mr. Wolfe crowed. He grinned at them. "I used to be pretty good when I was in school. Matter of fact, if I'd been a little taller, I might have played professionally."

"So you decided to become a murderer instead," Sarah mumbled under her breath.

Marvin gave her a warning look, but Mr. Wolfe had not heard her whispered remark. He smiled at Charlotte Graves. At this moment Mr. Wolfe seemed so nice, it was hard to remember what he'd done. But there was no use denying the facts. Marvin coughed nervously.

"That was good," he agreed, trying to keep his voice normal.

"Why don't we play the kids a game?" asked Charlotte Graves.

Before Marvin could think of a good escape, Mr. Wolfe shook his head. "We'll lose our reservations at the restaurant."

Suddenly a dark shadow swooped down almost to the ground and then darted away.

"Oh, yuck. A bat!" Sarah said, shuddering.

Mr. Wolfe grinned with a flash of bright teeth. "They're really fascinating creatures. I wonder where they are roosting now that I've chased them out of my attic?" he added, absently looking around.

"Not around here, I hope." Miss Graves looked nervous.

"We have to go in for dinner," Sarah said, checking the sky uneasily.

"We must get going, too. Maybe we can play basketball another time," Mr. Wolfe said.

"That would be great," Sarah and Marvin echoed without much enthusiasm.

Mr. Wolfe followed Miss Graves back to his house. But halfway across the driveway he turned back toward them. "Say, are you two going trick-or-treating this year?"

The question startled Marvin. When he nodded, Mr. Wolfe continued. "Halloween is my favorite holiday. Be sure and stop by my house. I have some friends I'd like you to meet. I think you'll find they are quite .. . ." He paused, as though looking for the right word. "Unusual," he added, finishing his sentence.

"Unusual?" Marvin croaked.

Mr. Wolfe stroked his beard. "I want you

two to be the first to see them. Miss Graves will be there, too."

"He probably wants to show us his collection of bodies," Marvin said glumly when Mr. Wolfe was out of hearing range.

"Do you think Miss Graves is in any danger?" Sarah asked. "She seems awfully nice."

"Mr. Wolfe seems to like her. Maybe she's one of them, too," Marvin answered. "Have you thought about her name—*Miss Graves*?" He tried to think of something cheerful but couldn't. "Whatever Mr. Wolfe's plans are for Halloween night, I'll bet it's bad news for us," he said grimly.

TEN

Mean ERNIE

On Monday afternoon Marvin stayed after school to help Mrs. Pfeiffer hang Halloween decorations around the room.

"Is anything bothering you?" Mrs. Pfeiffer asked kindly. "You've seemed very distracted lately."

Mrs. Pfeiffer was very small. In fact, she was not much bigger than some of her students. She looked sweet and always smelled of honeysuckle perfume. But the students in her fourth-grade room knew better than to misbehave. One look from Mrs. Pfeiffer's steely gray eyes and even Mean Ernie shrank.

Marvin taped a bright orange pumpkin to the door and stepped back to admire his work while he tried to think of an answer.

Mrs. Pfeiffer, he was sure, would listen very carefully to any stories about murders and missing bodies. Then she would immediately call his parents. "I've been worried about my report card," he finally blurted out.

"Why, Marvin," Mrs. Pfeiffer said, "you are one of my best students. There's no need for you to worry about grades."

She held up two black paper cats. "Which one would look better on the window?"

"That one looks scarier," he answered, pointing. He glanced at the clock. "I'd better go home," he said as he put on his jacket and zipped it.

"Thanks for all your help, dear," Mrs. Pfeiffer called after him as he dashed through the door.

Outside, he looked up the street for Sarah, but she was not in sight. She had raced home after school to get her camera, planning to take pictures of a large cocoon they'd noticed on the way to school. The photographs would be perfect for a science project she and her friend Laura were doing.

Much as he hated to admit it, Marvin felt safer walking home with Sarah. He pulled his notebook out of his pocket and concentrated on reading his notes as he walked. He didn't even notice Mean Ernie, who was leaning against a fence around the first street corner. Just as Marvin passed, Ernie's foot shot out, and

Marvin fell on the sidewalk with a splat, spilling papers, schoolbooks, and the notebook full of clues all over the sidewalk.

"Oh, excuse me," Mean Ernie said with exaggerated politeness. He offered Marvin a hand up. Without thinking, Marvin took it. Ernie pulled him halfway up and then let go before Marvin could get his balance. This time Marvin hit his elbow against the sidewalk when he fell.

"Oh, dear," Mean Ernie sneered. "I am so clumsy."

Marvin pulled himself up with as much dignity as he could muster. No one in the class liked Mean Ernie, but for some reason the bully had chosen Marvin for his special target. Marvin wished he would find someone else to pick on.

Ernie grabbed Marvin's notebook and started to thumb through the pages. "*Wolfman*," he read. "*Very strong. Likes bats. Buys Dracula clothes.* What's this all about, dweeb?"

"None of your business," Marvin said bravely. His mind was racing, trying to find a way to escape without losing his notebook.

A flicker of surprise flashed over Mean Ernie's face, but before he could speak, Sarah suddenly jumped over the fence. She tossed her camera to Marvin, grabbed Ernie's arm, and flipped him neatly facedown on the grass.

"Oww," Mean Ernie yelled. But Sarah held on and smiled as if she was a hunter posing for a picture. Marvin squinted through the viewfinder and squeezed the button.

Ernie was so busy yelling, he didn't even notice. "Are you going to leave Marvin alone?" Sarah asked.

"All right," Ernie mumbled. He twisted his body, trying to get loose from Sarah's grip.

"Promise?" Sarah asked sweetly.

"Yes," Mean Ernie roared. "Now let me up."

Sarah released her hold, and Ernie stood up and glared. Marvin wondered what Ernie would do now that he was free, but before he could find out, two teachers who lived near the school walked around the corner and gave them a curious glance as they passed. With a final glare, Mean Ernie dashed away down the street.

"I told you not to do that," Marvin said. "Now he'll tell everyone in school."

"No he won't," Sarah said cheerfully. She pointed to the camera. "He would have to admit that a girl got the best of him. And don't forget—we have the proof."

Marvin had the feeling Mean Ernie would find some way to get even in spite of Sarah's proof, but he tried not to worry about it as they walked home. Sarah went directly downstairs.

Photography was also Mr. Fremont's hobby, and he had walled in a small area of the basement to develop photographs. Although Marvin was not as interested, he did enjoy watching Sarah work in the dim reddish light of the darkroom. Sarah dipped the film into the small tubs of chemicals, and almost as if by magic the images slowly appeared. The pictures of the cocoon were crisp and clear, but it was the photograph of Ernie that made them both giggle.

"Perfect," Sarah exclaimed as she pinned them up to dry.

"All I'll have to do is threaten to pass that photo around," Marvin said gleefully. "Ernie would never want anyone to see a girl pinning him down on the ground."

"Wouldn't it be great if I could get evidence like that on Mr. Wolfe?" Sarah said. "I mean, a photograph that shows him doing something awful."

"I'll bet we could get plenty of evidence if we could see into the basement. We could sneak over there and look in a different window. Maybe he didn't cover them all," Marvin said. "This time we'll just be sure he's gone out."

After dinner, at his mother's insistence, Marvin struggled into his Frankenstein costume from the year before. "It's too tight," he complained. "I guess I just can't go trick-or-treating."

"Nonsense," said his mother. "I'll just let out this seam a little, and it will be fine." She took a few quick measurements. "My, you really have grown this last year."

Not enough, Marvin thought grimly, remembering his encounter with Ernie that afternoon. He imagined what it would be like to be six feet tall the next time he ran into Ernie. The thought almost made him smile.

ELEVEN

Marvin
TO THE
RESCUE

The next morning Sarah left for school early to walk with Laura. The picture of Ernie was in her pocket. "If Ernie tries anything, tell him to come to me," she said as she left the house.

Marvin decided it would still be safer not to run into Ernie. So he stood at the living room window, watching for the bully to pass the Fremonts' house on his way to school.

A yellow convertible pulled into Mr. Wolfe's driveway. Marvin went to another window, curious about who could be visiting so early. Frankie climbed out of the car and was soon busy repairing the porch with a hammer and nails. Marvin was relieved that Frankie's work did not seem to entail bodies of any sort.

"Why are you always so curious about Mr. Wolfe?" asked Mrs. Fremont, coming into the room.

"Mom, don't you think it's kind of strange that Mr. Wolfe never goes to work?" Marvin asked.

"He works at home," Mrs. Fremont answered. "He told me he develops computer programs." She patted Marvin's shoulder. "Are you still worried about that conversation in the parking lot? I'm sure you were too far away to hear correctly. Maybe Henry is someone they both work with. When the man said 'eliminate' he meant that Mr. Wolfe should *fire* Henry." Mrs. Fremont glanced at her watch. "Look at the time. You're going to be late for school, and I'm going to be late for work if we don't hurry."

At that moment Ernie walked by. Marvin slipped on his jacket, taking as much time as possible. When he reached the sidewalk, he checked to be sure Ernie was not waiting to trap him. But Ernie was already nearly a block ahead, walking quickly. His hands were stuffed in the pockets of his red coat, and he was hunched up against the cold. Marvin followed, carefully making sure to stay out of sight.

During silent reading, Mr. Grindstaff, the principal, came to the door and spoke with Mrs. Pfeiffer. Afterward she stood in front of the class with a serious look on her face.

"Mr. Grindstaff was on his way to a meeting

and discovered that someone has punctured holes in two of his tires. Does anyone remember seeing something suspicious in the teachers' parking lot this morning?"

"I saw Ernie there this morning," Melissa said loudly.

"Are you sure?" Mrs. Pfeiffer asked.

"I saw him, too," Aaron chimed in. "He was bending over, but I know it was him because of his bright red jacket."

"And yesterday he said he didn't like Mr. Grindstaff because he yelled at him for knocking one of the first graders down on the playground," Melissa added.

"It was an accident," Ernie protested. "I was running and I didn't see him. Mr. Grindstaff thought I did it on purpose."

"Ernie, were you in the parking lot this morning?" Mrs. Pfeiffer asked in an icy voice.

Marvin gulped. Here was a perfect chance to get even. Maybe Ernie hadn't punctured Mr. Grindstaff's tires, but he had certainly done a lot of other mean things. Ernie folded his arms across his chest and stared back defiantly. "I didn't do it" was all he said.

"I think you had better go talk to Mr. Grindstaff," Mrs. Pfeiffer told him.

Marvin sighed and stood up. "Ernie didn't do

it. I followed him all the way to school. He got here just before the bell rang. It must have been somebody else with a red coat." He glanced at Ernie. Mean Ernie stared back without a smile, but a flicker of respect showed in his eyes.

Mrs. Pfeiffer nodded. "Thank you, Marvin. It seems we owe Ernie an apology. It's never wise to jump to conclusions."

Later that morning the principal came and spoke quietly to Mrs. Pfeiffer.

"Mr. Grindstaff just informed me that there was a witness this morning. The culprit did have a red coat, but it was an older boy, high school age or older," Mrs. Pfeiffer explained when the principal had left.

At recess Ernie was waiting by the playground door. "Hey, I want to talk to you," he hissed as he grabbed Marvin's jacket and pulled him away from the crowd at the door.

Swallowing nervously, Marvin tried to look unafraid. "What about?"

"I want to know about that stuff you've got in your notebook."

This was so unexpected, Marvin's mouth fell open in surprise. All morning he had wondered what Ernie would do. He expected a thank-you, perhaps even a promise not to demand any more lunch-box treats. But Ernie did not even mention Marvin's coming to his defense.

"There've been some strange things happening next door," Marvin said. "I was just trying to figure them out."

"Strange? Like what?" Ernie demanded.

Reluctantly, Marvin told him about Mr. Wolfe. Ernie listened intently, his eyes bright.

"Little buddy, you don't really believe all that, do you?" Ernie said.

"It's true," Marvin protested.

Ernie shook his head. "I knew you were really weird. But Ernie always pays his debts. You saved my skin this morning, so I owe you one. I'll just hang around and help you solve this mystery. If this guy really is a murderer, you're going to need some protection."

"I don't need any help," Marvin insisted.

But Ernie did not seem to have heard. "Listen. You are pretty nice—but dumb. You had the perfect chance to get even with me, and you passed it up. A guy like you needs somebody to take care of him. And besides, I always wanted to work on a real mystery. I'd like to be a policeman when I grow up."

"You want to be a policeman?" Marvin asked.

Ernie scowled. "Is something wrong with that?"

"No-o," Marvin stammered. "I was thinking about being a detective myself."

Ernie grinned. "See, we have something in common. We're going to be great friends."

From the other side of the playground, Sarah had suddenly noticed Marvin talking to Ernie. She marched toward them. Marvin shook his head before she could show Ernie the picture. She stood a few feet away, watching carefully. Ernie did not seem to notice. He rubbed his hands together. "So, where do we start? If we do find anything suspicious, we can ask my uncle Ned for help. He's a real detective."

"W-we?" Marvin stammered.

"Sure." Ernie grinned again, and suddenly he didn't look mean at all. "You, me, and Sarah."

"You're not mad at Sarah for what she did?" Marvin asked.

Ernie shrugged. "I was, at first." Then an unexpected smile crossed his face. "Do you think if we were friends she would teach me that trick? Then the kids would *really* be afraid of me."

TWELVE

Monster
MUSIC

Ernie kept his promise. For the rest of the day, no matter how much Marvin protested, Ernie was there. When Richard crowded in line ahead of Marvin on the way to the lunchroom, Ernie was there, glowering until Richard sneaked back to the end of the line. When Josh threw the basketball wildly and it hit Marvin in the back, Ernie threatened to beat him to a pulp. Marvin had to explain three times that it was only an accident. Even then Ernie didn't give up. "There better not be any more accidents," he growled. "No one touches my little buddy."

"What is going on?" Sarah asked on the playground. "Ernie's telling everyone he's your best friend."

Marvin groaned. "He thinks he owes me a favor," he said. He explained quickly just as Ernie caught up with him again.

"Everyone's going to be afraid of me," Marvin pleaded as Ernie walked him home from school. "I don't want a bodyguard."

"You did me a favor. When someone does me a favor, I do them a favor," Ernie insisted. "I've got a plan," he added. "When Mr. Wolfe leaves tonight, we'll sneak over and peek into his basement."

Marvin and Sarah exchanged a look.

"We already tried that," Sarah said quickly. "We couldn't see through the curtains."

Ernie shrugged. "Then we'll have to think of something else. I'll be over by six o'clock."

Marvin hoped Ernie wouldn't show up, but promptly at six o'clock that night the doorbell rang. Marvin and Sarah had just finished dinner, and Mrs. Fremont was working on Marvin's costume. She had already added material to make the arms longer. Now she was stuffing a pouch in the back to make a hump.

"Hi, little buddy," Ernie said with a wide grin. "Ready for a little detective work?" he whispered.

Mrs. Fremont's eyes widened when she learned that this was Mean Ernie, but Marvin hastened to reassure her.

"We're just going to play basketball," Marvin explained.

"Don't you worry about Marvin when he's with me," Ernie told her. "I take real good care of my friends."

Mrs. Fremont gave Marvin a "you must explain all this to me later" look, but she managed a weak smile, then went back to her sewing. "Put your coats on; it's pretty cold."

It was chilly—and dark. Although Mr. Fremont had installed a spotlight for the basketball hoop, the area outside of the light was shadowy and ominously quiet. A brisk wind blew dry leaves across the pavement with a *skritch-skritch*. In spite of his warm jacket, Marvin felt cold.

"It sure is dark next door," Sarah remarked.

Mr. Wolfe's house was completely shrouded in darkness except for a little circle of light around the basement window.

"Well," said Ernie a little too loudly. "That's good. Now no one will see us."

Uneasily they began a halfhearted game of basketball, waiting for Mr. Wolfe to leave. Suddenly Ernie grabbed Marvin's arm and yelped, "What's that?"

From Mr. Wolfe's house came the faint sound of music, but it was unlike anything they had ever heard. This music was a strange and spooky mixture of sounds between a moan and a wail. Then suddenly the music stopped, and they heard something even worse. Sarah's eyes grew round with fear. Even Ernie's freckles stood out against his white face as a wild cackling laughter floated across the darkness and surrounded them. Marvin's knees quivered, but he seemed firmly rooted to the spot, unable to make himself move. Then, just as abruptly as it had started, the noise stopped. A minute later the basement light snapped off, and a dark silence settled over Mr. Wolfe's house.

Then Mr. Wolfe came out of the back door. He waved as he walked quickly to his garage, and a moment later his car sped away down the street.

THIRTEEN

More Bodies
IN THE
BASEMENT

Ernie was the first to find his voice. "Well, I guess this is our chance to find a window we can see into," he said, not very eagerly.

"What do you suppose that laughing was all about?" Sarah asked in a hushed voice.

"Mr. Wolfe probably just murdered somebody else," Marvin said glumly.

They crouched beside some bushes. No one wanted to make the first move toward the house. Finally Marvin sighed. "If we don't hurry up, Mr. Wolfe will be back."

"Or Mom or Dad will check up on us. They would be very unhappy to find us spying on a neighbor," Sarah said.

"How are we going to see into the house?" Marvin asked. "Mr. Wolfe turned off all the lights."

Ernie reached in his pocket and pulled out a small flashlight. "I thought of that before I left home."

Slowly they crossed the space between the houses. From inside Mr. Wolfe's house they could make out wild barking. Ernie looked dismayed, but Marvin smiled. "Quiet, Jack," he called softly as he climbed the steps to the porch. Jack's barking stopped, and he whined a softer greeting. Somehow Jack's presence made them all feel better.

Ernie examined the house. A porch ran partway across the front. There was a large window to one side of the door, but the drapes were closed. "Let's check through that other window," he said. He ran down the porch steps and stood below a small window that was at least eight feet off the ground. There was some lumber piled beneath it from Frankie's repairs. But even standing on tiptoe on the stack of lumber, Ernie was not tall enough to peer in.

"I thought we were going to check out the basement," Sarah protested.

"It sounded to me like those noises came from upstairs," Ernie whispered.

"He's right," Marvin answered. "But how are we going to see in? We need a ladder."

"I have an idea," Ernie said. "I'll kneel down on one knee. Then you can stand on the other one and reach."

Marvin stepped up as gently as he could and gingerly balanced himself on the side of the house. "Are you okay?" he asked hoarsely.

"Yes, but hurry up," Ernie said with a gasp. "You're heavy."

Marvin cupped his hands and peered in through the glass. "I can't see anything," he reported. "I need the flashlight."

Ernie groped in his pocket for the light. But before he could hand it to Marvin, his knee gave out. Both boys tumbled down. "Ow," Ernie groaned, pushing Marvin off. From inside the house came the sound of Jack barking wildly.

"I'm the one who fell the farthest," Marvin said, rubbing his knee and forgetting to whisper.

"Yeah, but you landed on me," Ernie said.

Sarah stood over them, her hands on her hips. "Jeepers. If you two don't stop making so much noise, the whole neighborhood is going to hear you."

Instantly the boys stopped moaning. "She's right," Marvin said. "Let's see if we can get a look in any of the basement windows."

"I'll do it," Sarah said. She grabbed the flash–

light and marched around to the back of the house. The boys followed meekly.

This window was also covered, but the curtains were open a tiny slit. Sarah flashed the light through. "I don't see . . . ," Sarah said. Then she snapped off the light, but not before the boys saw her pale face. "Let's get out of here," she said, already running back to the safety of the Fremonts' yard.

Marvin and Ernie stumbled behind her. Marvin grabbed Sarah's arm. "What is it? What did you see?" he asked.

"There were people in there," Sarah gasped. She looked nervously back at the house to make sure they weren't being followed.

"In the dark?" Ernie asked.

Sarah sounded calmer now. "I didn't see their faces, but I could see a couch, and there were at least three pairs of shoes in front of it."

"Oh," Ernie scoffed. "Maybe Mr. Wolfe just lines his shoes up there to make it easy to find them."

Sarah gave Ernie a withering look. "In the basement? And anyway, there were *legs* in them, dummy." She paused and took a deep breath. "There was something else. I saw a body facedown on the floor."

They sat together, huddled in the warm glow from the light on the Fremonts' back porch. Marvin pulled his notebook out of his pocket. "Why would three people be sitting in the dark with a dead body?" he asked as he jotted down Sarah's report.

"I don't know, and I don't think I want to find out," Ernie said. "I thought this was just a game. I didn't know you were chasing real murderers. Being friends with you two is dangerous."

"You didn't have to help us," Marvin said sharply. "You've done enough today. Let's just say we're even, and you can go home."

Ernie looked hurt, and Sarah stepped between them. "Jeepers," she said, putting her hands on her hips. "Why don't you two forget about favors and just be friends?"

Ernie suddenly looked shy. "I'd like that," Marvin told him, realizing it was true.

But Sarah wasn't finished. "You know, Ernie, you are pretty nice when you try. So why were you so mean before?"

Ernie hung his head. "I don't know. I always liked you and Marvin. But you never even talked to me except when I bugged you. Then Marvin stuck up for me even though I'd been so awful, so I figured we could be friends after all."

Sarah reached in her pocket and pulled out a crumpled picture. "If we're going to be friends, I guess we don't need this." She handed him the picture Marvin had taken of her pinning Ernie to the ground.

For a second Ernie looked angry. Then a slow grin spread across his face. "I'm glad you didn't show this to anyone else," he said as he stuffed it into his pocket.

Marvin reread the clues he'd written in his notebook. "It doesn't make sense. Why would three people be sitting in the dark with a dead body? Maybe we should take another look."

"I know what I saw," Sarah said stubbornly.

"Yikes," Ernie gasped. "Mr. Wolfe is back." As the car pulled up the length of driveway, the three detectives dived into the darkness of the nearby bushes.

"Hey, he's got Miss Graves with him," Marvin whispered as the car doors opened.

Charlotte Graves's voice floated across the driveway. "So a few more days of that, and Henry will do anything we want," Miss Graves said.

"I hope you didn't have to mess him up very much," answered Mr. Wolfe.

"Just a little cut on the back of the neck," Miss Graves said cheerfully.

"I still don't think he will be any match for Dracula," Mr. Wolfe continued as they walked in the door. "Poor old Henry. I really liked him, but . . ." The rest of his sentence was inaudible as they walked into the house and the door swung closed.

At first, nobody could speak. "Now we know why no one has found the body," Sarah said at last. "Henry must have been unconscious that night. Frankie drove him to Miss Graves's house. Now she's holding Henry prisoner, and Dracula is helping her torture him!"

The three friends stared at one another in horror.

FOURTEEN

Bats
IN THE
NEIGHBORHOOD

"That's why Miss Graves didn't know about the mound builders," Marvin said. "I'll bet she isn't really an archaeologist at all."

"She seemed so nice," Sarah said. "I can't believe she'd be friends with someone like Frankie."

"Maybe she's not. Maybe he was just sort of a delivery person," Marvin said thoughtfully.

"We have to tell someone," Sarah said firmly.

"We don't even know what's going on," Marvin pointed out glumly. "And I bet that evidence in the basement will disappear as fast as Henry did."

"Maybe Marvin is right," Ernie said excitedly. "Maybe Mr. Wolfe *is* a werewolf. On Halloween night he and Dracula are going to take over the whole town. But Henry found out, so they are trying to turn him into some kind of zombie or something. . . ." His voice trailed off.

"That wouldn't work," Marvin said. "There are fifteen thousand people in Liberty Corners. Even Dracula couldn't bite that many people in one night. Second, who are Mr. Fiumera and the man I overheard talking to Mr. Wolfe?"

Sarah snapped her fingers. "My camera!" she exclaimed. "If we knew where Miss Graves lived, we could snoop around. We could talk to her neighbors and find out if they've noticed anything suspicious. Or maybe we could even peek in her house, and I could get a picture of poor Henry."

"Everyone would have to believe us then," Ernie said. Then he jumped up. "I have an even better idea. We find out where Miss Graves lives, and the next time she visits Mr. Wolfe, we could sneak over and rescue Henry."

Marvin got up from behind the bushes. "We don't know where she lives," he said finally.

"Phone book!" Sarah shouted.

She started to go in the house to fetch it, but Marvin shook his head. "She said she just moved here. She wouldn't be in the phone book."

"I'll bet my uncle Ned could help," Ernie said. "Why don't you ask your parents if you can go with me to the police station after school? Just tell them it's research for a report."

The next morning Marvin and Sarah had another shock. Just as they walked out their door to go to school, Frankie pulled into Mr. Wolfe's driveway in a bright red foreign car. Glowering as usual, he unloaded several small wooden boxes. "Bat houses," he grumbled when he noticed the children staring. "Did you ever hear of anything so dumb?"

Before they could answer, Mr. Wolfe opened his front door. "Oh, good, you've finished them," he said. "Did you follow the measurements I gave you?"

Frankie nodded sourly. "Never built a bat house before," he grumbled.

"Bats are a hobby of mine," Mr. Wolfe said cheerfully. "Since I chased them out of their old houses, the least I could do was make them some new ones."

"Do you still think Mr. Wolfe is just an ordinary person?" Marvin demanded as they hurried toward school. "Halloween is probably a special day for vampires and werewolves. That's only two days away. If we don't rescue Henry pretty soon, I have a dreadful feeling it will be too late."

By the time Marvin got to his classroom,

Mrs. Pfeiffer was already writing math problems on the blackboard. As soon as the lesson was over she took a book from her desk. The cover was illustrated with a wispy ghost with red eyes standing behind some unsuspecting children. "With Halloween so near, I thought you might enjoy some good ghost stories," she said as she started to read.

Everyone in class listened intently. Mrs. Pfeiffer was a good reader. She read in a soft spooky voice that made shivers go up Marvin's back. He exchanged a glance with Ernie. They didn't need to hear a scary story. They were living through one.

The day seemed to drag on forever, but at last the bell rang.

Sarah met them on the playground, and they started out together.

"I called my uncle Ned," Ernie said. "He said it was okay for us to go over there. Have you ever been to the police station?"

"We took a tour in kindergarten," Marvin said.

"Uncle Ned is one of the best detectives," Ernie bragged.

"Do you think he'll believe us?" Marvin asked.

"Maybe we shouldn't say anything about

werewolves," Ernie said thoughtfully. "You could just pretend to be interested in police work. Then mention the conversation you heard, and about seeing Frankie carrying Henry."

"And about the other body I saw in the basement," Sarah added.

"That might be a little too much. If Uncle Ned thinks we're just being weird, we'll rescue Henry by ourselves. He'll have to believe us then."

"We still don't know where Miss Graves lives," Sarah pointed out.

Ernie grinned. "Don't worry about it. I've got it all figured out." He pulled a scrap of paper out of his pocket. "Uncle Ned is not the only good detective in the family."

"What's that?" Marvin and Sarah asked together.

"Miss Gráves's license number," Ernie crowed. "Last night Mom realized that there wasn't enough milk for breakfast. So we went to McNaulty's to get some. When we stopped at the stop sign, there was Miss Graves parked right near the alley by Frankie's garage. So I wrote down her license number."

"What was she doing by Frankie's garage?" Marvin asked.

Ernie shrugged. "Beats me. She was just sitting in her car, staring out the window at Frankie's. She didn't even notice me."

"I'll bet she's watching Frankie to make sure he doesn't tell about Henry," Marvin said.

Sarah and Marvin followed Ernie through the door of the police station. They were in a room that looked like an ordinary office except for the dispatcher, who was listening to a crackling radio in one corner. He looked up when they came in and waved. "Hi, Ernie. Your uncle's expecting you. Go on back."

Ernie led the way to a larger room where there was a lot more activity. Several people were busy typing reports at some battered desks stacked high with papers. In one corner a white-haired man was talking to a uniformed police officer. Ernie waved at several people as he made his way to a small private office.

"How's my favorite nephew?" Uncle Ned was a big man with a ruddy complexion, a large nose, and laugh lines around his eyes. Marvin liked him instantly.

"This is my little buddy, Marvin, and his sister, Sarah. I hoped you could show them around," Ernie explained. "They're interested in how crimes are solved."

Uncle Ned pushed aside a stack of papers.

"It's not like you see on television. A lot of what we do is paperwork," he said.

"I'd still like to be a detective when I grow up," Marvin said. "I might call myself Marvelous Marvin."

"Catchy name," said Uncle Ned. He took them to a small room. "This is where we fingerprint people after we arrest them. Do you know about fingerprints?"

Marvin nodded. "I've seen that on television. Everyone has different fingerprints. If you find some at the scene of a crime, you run them through a computer, hoping to find a match."

"Of course that only works if they've been fingerprinted before, so that they're on file. But we can match them to a suspect when we bring one in."

"We know all that," Ernie said, trying to sound casual. "But I was wondering about license plates. If you have a number, how long does it take to find out whose it is?"

"Just a couple of minutes," Uncle Ned answered. "We just type the information into the computer, and a minute later we have a name."

"I wrote down the number of a car I saw last night," Ernie said. "Could you show us how it works?"

Uncle Ned hesitated. "I guess it couldn't do any harm." He typed the numbers on the keyboard, and a minute later they had their answer: *Charlotte Sweet. 707 Main Street.* Uncle Ned looked at the name again and frowned. "How did you say you got this number?"

"It was just a car I saw parked on the road," Ernie said innocently. "Why? Who is Charlotte Sweet?"

"Charlotte Sweet works right here," answered Uncle Ned. "She is one of Liberty Corners's best detectives."

FIFTEEN

Marvin
SPOTS
A CLUE

"We never told Uncle Ned about our suspicions," Ernie said when they were back on the street.

"I needed time to think," Marvin said. "There are two possibilities. One is that the police are already onto Mr. Wolfe. In that case, we should tell Charlotte what we know."

"She must be pretending to be his girlfriend so she can investigate him," Sarah said.

"Then what is she doing with Henry?" Ernie demanded.

"Maybe she's trying to make Mr. Wolfe think she's a criminal, too, so that he'll tell her about all the people he's murdered," Marvin said.

"Hey," Ernie said. "You said two possibilities. What's number two?"

"That Charlotte really is helping Mr. Wolfe.

If we told your uncle, she'd be sure to find out. We might disappear just like Henry."

"I vote for her being a real detective," Sarah said.

"I think so, too," Marvin agreed.

"We've got her address," Ernie pointed out. "Maybe we should go talk to her."

They had reached the crosswalk and stood waiting for the light to change. Just before the light turned green, a small black sports car zoomed through the intersection. Marvin just caught a glimpse of Frankie hunched over the wheel. Marvin's eyes widened, and he watched the car proceed down the road.

"Did you notice anything strange about that car Frankie was driving?" Marvin asked.

Ernie shrugged. "It was just a fancy sports car."

"Except for the color, it's exactly like Mrs. Hanson's," Marvin replied.

Sarah and Ernie stared intently after the rapidly moving car. "Did it have a dent in the fender?" Sarah asked.

"I couldn't see," Marvin admitted. "But I'm sure that's Mrs. Hanson's car. Maybe Frankie stole it. Then he might have fixed the dent and painted the car to disguise it."

They crossed the intersection. Marvin

stopped in the middle of the sidewalk and snapped his fingers. "Remember that day we were following Mr. Wolfe? We saw Frankie with yellow paint on him. He acted upset because we were near his garage. And a couple of days later he was driving a yellow car."

"That's right." Sarah nodded. "Frankie always seems to have a lot of different cars."

Marvin looked thoughtful. "I'll bet Frankie is part of a stolen-car gang."

Ernie nodded. "If that's true, there is bound to be some evidence in that garage."

"Oh no," Sarah groaned. "We don't need another mystery. Why don't we just tell your uncle? Or Detective Sweet," she added brightly. "Remember, you saw her parked by Frankie's garage. Maybe she already suspects him."

Ernie shook his head stubbornly. "Uncle Ned told me once that the police can't just barge into your house and look for clues. They have to have some evidence first. Then they can get a warrant. That's a paper that says they can go in and investigate. But we might be able to find some evidence and save them all that work."

"Ernie's right," Marvin said. "Frankie was heading away from his house. He'll probably be gone for a while. We're only a few blocks away from the garage. If we hurry, we could take a quick peek around. Then we'll tell Miss Sweet what we found."

Sarah shook her head, looking worried. "I have a feeling this is a bad idea, but if we're going to do it, we'd better hurry."

They raced down the street. Then, taking a quick glance back to reassure themselves that Frankie was not in sight, they ducked down the alley behind Frankie's garage.

SIXTEEN

TRAPPED!

The only windows in Frankie's garage were three very small panes just below the roof. A high wooden fence encircled the small backyard, and there was a gate at one side.

Ernie pulled at the handle of one of the overhead doors, but it was tightly locked.

"Now what?" asked Sarah. "There's no way we could see in those windows."

"Let's walk around the building," Marvin said. "Maybe there's another way in."

The rusty gate was unlocked. It swung open with a groaning squeak at Marvin's touch. Exchanging uneasy but determined glances, they entered the yard and pulled the gate closed behind them.

The area inside the gate looked more like a junk heap than a backyard. Piles of tires, wood scraps, and auto parts were everywhere. Gingerly stepping over the debris, Marvin led the way to a small door at the back of the garage and tried the handle.

"It's unlocked," he exclaimed.

Sarah glanced over her shoulder nervously. "Let's take a peek and get out of here. It's getting dark, and I sure don't want to be here when Frankie returns."

"What sort of things should we look for, little buddy?" Ernie asked.

Marvin peered into the gloom of the almost-dark garage. "I don't know," he admitted with a sheepish shrug. "Clues."

Sarah was already poking around some of the barrels and boxes stacked around the walls. "How's this for a clue?" she said, bending over a cardboard box.

The boys hurried over to look. Inside were at least a dozen license plates. Ernie started to grab one, but Marvin stopped him.

"They probably have a lot of fingerprints on them," he said. "I wonder if one of them belongs to Mrs. Hanson."

The garage floor was sprinkled with drops of different colors of paint. Marvin pointed to an air compressor with a spray attachment. Drops of black paint still clung to the nozzle. "That's what he uses to paint the cars."

"I think we'd better get out of here and tell Detective Sweet what we've seen," Sarah said.

Marvin nodded. But before they could move, they heard the sound of a car moving down the alley. The car stopped in front of the garage, and a door slammed.

"Quick, get behind there," Ernie hissed as the sound of shoes crunching across the gravel reached them. They dived desperately behind several large barrels, scrunching down to make themselves as small as possible.

Marvin heard a key turn in the lock, and a second later the door slid up. Venturing a quick glance over the top of the barrel, Marvin saw Frankie standing by the open door. Frankie was staring into the garage, looking puzzled. Then he frowned.

Silently, Ernie hit his head with his palm and pointed to the back of the garage. Marvin's stomach gave a lurch as he realized what Ernie was trying to tell him. They had forgotten to close the back door.

SEVENTEEN

CAUGHT!

"Who's in here?" Frankie growled. He walked a few feet into the garage and kicked at some boxes. Only a few more feet and he would reach the barrels.

Then, just as Marvin felt he would explode from holding his breath, a second car could be heard turning into the alley. With a grunt, Frankie stepped back outside just as two men drove up in a truck that was pulling a large trailer.

The driver of the truck sounded angry. "Hey, Frankie. Where did you get this car? Are you going into business for yourself now?"

"N–no," Frankie stammered. "I was going to give it to you, Sly. Honest. I was just trying to help you out."

"Listen, dummy," growled the man called Sly. "A car like this is easy to spot in a small town. That's why we unload them in the city. Your job is to paint them. Nothing else. Understand?"

"Why is the car in the alley?" asked the other man.

"I was just taking it out for a test drive." Frankie's voice sounded nervous. "When I came back, I found the back door open. I was just checking around."

Sly stepped out of the truck, and Marvin risked another peek. The man was very wide and very tall, so he towered over Frankie. "You hear that, Rick?" the big man said in a growling voice. "He took the car out for a test drive."

"I heard that, Sly," the second man agreed. "That's a pretty dumb thing to do," he said to Frankie.

"Are you trying to get us caught?" Sly asked.

"N–no," Frankie stammered. "I just wanted to see how it drove. Nobody would recognize it. I changed the color."

"Listen, dummy," Sly said, "I don't care how much you changed the color. Someone could notice. We steal the cars. You paint them and hide them until we pick them up."

Frankie nodded miserably. "It won't happen again."

"It better not. Now help us load the trailer."

"I better check around and find out why the door was open," Frankie insisted.

"You probably forgot to close it tight," Sly said. "Just like you forgot you weren't supposed to drive the cars. Now get out here and help us."

"As soon as Frankie gets in the car, go out the back door," Marvin whispered. "We can hide in the yard until they've gone."

"Why not stay here?" Sarah asked quietly.

Ernie shook his head. "Marvin's right. Frankie will search the garage as soon as those other two are gone. Our best chance is to make a run for it."

From the alley they heard Sly shouting orders. Rick backed the truck in line with the car, blocking the garage door and shielding Marvin, Sarah, and Ernie from view. "Here's our chance," Marvin whispered, easing out from behind the barrels. They hurried to the still-open back door and slipped out into the yard.

"Behind that stack of tires would be a good place," Sarah whispered urgently.

As they hurried across the yard, Marvin tripped over a large piece of steel, which fell against some of the other debris with a clang. Marvin stopped, frozen with shock over the sudden loud noise. But the men didn't seem to have heard it over the noise of the truck's engine.

Marvin's ankle was beginning to throb. Limping, he headed for the tire stack to join the others. He had almost made it when a large hand suddenly fell on his shoulder. "I knew I shut that door," Frankie said. "I should have guessed who it was, you little snoop."

EIGHTEEN

A Daring
RESCUE

Marvin twisted under Frankie's rough grasp. "Let me go, you crook."

Frankie laughed unpleasantly. "I don't think so. I want you to meet a couple of friends of mine."

Marvin realized that Ernie and Sarah had reached the safety of the tire stack before Frankie had seen them. For a moment he felt hopeful that they could escape and get help. But a second later Ernie charged around the tires and made a flying tackle at Frankie. "You let my little buddy go," he yelled. Startled, Frankie let go of Marvin. Then Sarah ran out with a wild karate kick at his knee that sent Frankie sprawling on the ground.

"Let's get out of here," Ernie yelled, grabbing Marvin's arm to support him as he limped for the gate. Frankie was still struggling to his feet.

But the way was blocked by Sly and Rick, who had heard the commotion and hurried around to investigate.

"Through the garage," Sarah shouted, changing directions. They raced through the door and squeezed around the truck before the men reached them.

"Get them," Frankie shouted.

"You get them," Sly yelled. "We're getting out of here." He and Rick jumped in the truck and gunned the motor.

Ernie and Sarah raced down the alley, half-dragging Marvin. The truck was right behind them. Once they reached the busy street, Marvin was reasonably sure they'd be safe. There were too many cars going by for Frankie to grab them. Then suddenly he heard the sound of sirens. A police car skidded to a stop, blocking the alley, and two police officers jumped out.

Sly jammed on the brakes and put the truck in reverse. But a second police car pulled across the other end of the alley.

"Wow," shouted Ernie as a police officer hustled them to safety behind the squad car. "This is the greatest thing I've ever seen."

Surrounded, Sly and Rick climbed glumly

from the truck. An officer was already hand-cuffing a subdued Frankie. By now several other police cars had pulled up. Detective Sweet stepped out of one of them. She talked briefly with one of the officers and then walked over to where Marvin, Sarah, and Ernie were waiting. "Well," she said sternly, "you three almost got yourselves in a mess."

Everyone started talking at once. Finally Marvin held up his hand. "I saw Frankie driving a car that I was pretty sure was Mrs. Hanson's. We thought you would need some evidence, so we investigated his garage. But then Frankie came back."

"I've known for some time that Frankie was part of a car-theft ring," Detective Sweet explained, still looking stern.

"You knew?" Ernie exclaimed. "Then why didn't you arrest him?"

"We wanted to catch the whole gang togeth-er," Detective Sweet said. "I pretended that I was a college professor and that I'd just moved to town. I had Frankie repair my car, hoping he would steal it." She chuckled. "I guess he liked Mrs. Hanson's car better than mine. These three are just part of a ring of car thieves that have been operating all over the state. We've been watching Frankie's house. That's why I saw you sneak into the garage. You almost fouled up weeks of investigation."

Marvin dug his toe into the gravel. "Sorry. We were trying to help."

"Luckily we were almost ready to strike anyway," Detective Sweet said, softening a little. "Right this minute the rest of the gang is being arrested. But next time, leave the police work to us."

"Does Mr. Wolfe know who you really are?" Sarah asked.

Detective Sweet shook her head. "I couldn't risk anyone in the neighborhood knowing I am a detective. I'll tell him tonight."

"We thought you were investigating Mr. Wolfe," Marvin admitted.

"Why would I want to investigate Mr. Wolfe?" Detective Sweet asked. "He's a very nice man."

Marvin felt his face grow hot. "Two weeks ago I overheard Mr. Wolfe talking about getting rid of somebody named Henry."

"You know about Henry," Ernie said accusingly. "We know Frankie took him to you. We heard you talking about Henry to Mr. Wolfe."

"And Mr. Wolfe murdered someone else, too.

I saw the body on his basement floor," Sarah added.

"Murdered?" For a second Detective Sweet looked startled. Then she smiled slightly. "I'm pretty busy right now. But if you meet me Friday night at Mr. Wolfe's house, you'll understand everything. In the meantime, no more police work for you three."

Detective Sweet walked back to where the officers were putting Frankie and his friends in the squad car to take them to the police station. Halfway to the car she turned around. Her smile was gone, and her voice sounded strange and ominous. "The day after tomorrow is Halloween. Mr. Wolfe is really anxious to see you all."

NINETEEN

HALLOWEEN

The weather was perfect for Halloween. Even so, Marvin and Sarah were not eager to leave the safety of their house. They had not seen Detective Sweet or Mr. Wolfe all day, although Sarah was sure she had heard someone groaning in Mr. Wolfe's house after school.

"It's strange Detective Sweet hasn't talked to us about Mr. Wolfe," Sarah said. "You would think she would have wanted to ask us some questions after we told her about the murder plot."

"Maybe she already knew the answers," Marvin said soberly.

"What do you mean?" asked Sarah.

"Well, she really is a good detective. But she has been spending a lot of time at Mr. Wolfe's house. Do you know what happens if you are bitten by a werewolf?" Marvin answered his own question. "You turn into a werewolf yourself."

"We still haven't found Henry," Sarah reminded him. "Or figured out why Mr. Wolfe was buying clothes for Dracula."

"We'll have to go trick-or-treating at Mr. Wolfe's house," Marvin said. "It's our only chance to find out what's going on. Then we'll have something to tell Ernie's uncle Ned. Maybe since we are sort of celebrities, he will believe us."

They had become celebrities after their adventures were reported on the late-night news and again in the paper. Mr. Grindstaff had called a special assembly for them to tell the story to the whole school. Several kids cheered when they got to the part about Sarah and Ernie charging Frankie, and afterward some of the older boys asked Ernie and Marvin to play football at recess.

But Mr. and Mrs. Fremont had not been happy over their adventures. "I can't believe you would do anything so dangerous," Mrs. Fremont had scolded. "I should keep you home instead of letting you go trick-or-treating."

Marvin felt hopeful for the first time that

day. "You're right, Mom. That was a dumb thing to do. We should not be allowed to trick-or-treat."

Mrs. Fremont's face softened. "Well, as long as you realize how foolish you were. Mrs. Hanson is thrilled that she'll get her car back, even if it is a different color. And Mr. Wolfe really wants you to stop by. He has fixed up a surprise for all the kids in the neighborhood, sort of a housewarming. But he told me he wants you two to be the first. So I'll let it go this time. But never again. Do you hear me?"

Marvin nodded weakly. "Is it okay if Ernie goes with us?"

Mrs. Fremont smiled. Ever since she had heard how Ernie had tackled Frankie to save Marvin, she had been telling everyone how wonderful he was. "Of course," she said.

Just at dark, Ernie knocked at the door, wearing a clown suit with baggy pants and a red nose.

"Don't you dare laugh." Ernie glowered. "My mother made it."

"Actually, I think it looks pretty good," Sarah told him. "Let's go before everyone runs out of candy."

"Remember, no eating until we look it over," Mr. Fremont called from the kitchen.

"We won't," they all promised as they walked out the door.

Sarah looked brave enough in her Super-woman costume, but as soon as they were outside she grabbed Marvin's arm.

"Maybe we should think about this," she whispered, even though no one was near.

"We have to go," Marvin said, trying to hide his own uneasiness. "If we don't show up, Mr. Wolfe might suspect that we know about him."

Sarah sighed. "I really want to be a photographer when I grow up, *not* a werewolf."

Marvin looked at Mr. Wolfe's house and shivered, in spite of the warm breeze.

"We'll just stay on the porch. He wouldn't dare do anything with so many people around," Sarah said. She pointed to the groups of children up and down the street.

"No," Ernie said, shaking his head. "We need to get inside—to see if there're more clues. You know, like puddles of blood. Maybe while Detective Sweet is talking, one of us will get a chance to sneak to the basement."

With a shaking finger, Marvin rang the bell.

From inside the house came spooky music and a scraping noise that sounded like chains being dragged across the floor. Ernie took a step backward, nearly falling off the porch. Suddenly the door was flung open by an ugly woman with a warty nose who was dressed in a long black dress and a witch's hat. Her long fingernails were painted bright red—blood red.

"Trick or treat," Marvin managed to croak out. Behind him he heard Sarah gasp.

"Is that Marvin and Sarah?" Mr. Wolfe rose from the sofa. Marvin could see into the living room, where the only light came from some flickering candles on a table.

Mr. Wolfe seemed to have grown a longer beard and very hairy hands since the last time Marvin had seen him. But he was too busy looking at the rest of the room's occupants to think about it. Clustered around an old record player, listening to the awful music, was every horrible creature Marvin could have imagined in his worst dreams. Monsters and goblins, and even Frankenstein's monster and Dracula, all sat watching as Mr. Wolfe walked to the door.

TWENTY

DRACULA

"Don't you want to come in and meet my friends?" When Mr. Wolfe smiled, Marvin noticed he had very pointy teeth. He waved one hairy hand toward the couch. "We've been waiting for you," he growled.

"Jeepers. Let's get out of here," Sarah whispered. Ernie pulled at his arm, but Marvin remained frozen in one spot. Then his frightened look melted away and was replaced with a smile. A good detective is trained to notice details, he told himself.

With one hand he grabbed for Sarah just as she started to jump off the porch steps. With the other he pointed into the room. "They're dummies—Dracula and all the monsters. They're fake!"

Mr. Wolfe looked disappointed.

"I was hoping they'd fool you longer than that," the witch said in Charlotte Sweet's voice. She had taken a seat next to Frankenstein.

"They are very good," Marvin admitted. "But a good detective is hard to fool. And I am"—he smiled modestly—"a very good detective."

"That's what Charlotte told me," Mr. Wolfe replied. "I knew Frankie wasn't a very likable fellow, but I never suspected he was a crook." He smiled at Detective Sweet. "I guess I wouldn't be a very good detective. I didn't even know Miss Graves was not Charlotte's name."

Mr. Wolfe paused to greet a bunch of trick-or-treaters. "Come in, come in," he called heartily to the parents. "I've been wanting to meet some of my neighbors."

Miss Sweet passed out treats to the children. Soon the house was filled with happy laughter as children and parents bobbed for apples, drew faces on jack-o'-lanterns, played pin the legs on the spider, and admired Dracula.

When the first group had left, Marvin laughed. "We saw you and Frankie carry something out of your house late one night. Was it by any chance one of the dummies?"

Mr. Wolfe looked puzzled. Then he too began

to laugh. "I never thought how it would look if anyone saw us."

"At first I wondered why no one ever found the body," Marvin said. "Then later we thought Miss Sweet was torturing him."

"Torturing?" Mr. Wolfe looked puzzled.

"We heard you talking the other night when you came home," Sarah explained. "You were talking about cutting Henry's neck to make him do what you wanted."

Mr. Wolfe laughed heartily. "You *are* good detectives," he said.

"Why do you have your house full of dummies?" Ernie asked, still sounding suspicious.

"They're not really dummies," Mr. Wolfe explained. "Actually, they are more like robots. They're controlled with a computer." He flipped a switch on a small black box, and Dracula suddenly came to life, standing up and lurching menacingly across the room. "I want to suck your blood," the Dracula robot said in a chilling voice.

Mr. Wolfe used the black box to send Dracula back to his chair. "I work for the McGreggor Toy Company. I invent toys," explained Mr. Wolfe. "Mostly I do robots, spaceships, that sort of thing. There are computerized life-size dummies already. But I invented a new program that makes them able to do many more things and move almost like real people. They can even hold a simple conversation. I've been working on them for a long time."

"Who would want one?" Sarah asked, peering closely at the life-size figures as though she still expected them to come to life.

Mr. Wolfe laughed again. "They don't all look like that. I just dressed them that way to have a little fun. Actually, Dracula's already been sold to an amusement park. He'll scare people in the fun house. This one here," he added, taking a mask off a ghostly-looking creature to reveal an ordinary face underneath, "will be a blacksmith in a western village. As the train chugs by, he'll use the bellows to build up his fire and pound on a horseshoe just like a real blacksmith might have done. If they are a success, Mr. Fiumera, the amusement park owner, is going to buy enough to populate the whole town."

Mr. Wolfe paused long enough to pass out some treats to some wide-eyed children who had come to the door. The children took the treats and left quickly.

"Oh, dear. We're forgetting the music," Detective Sweet said. She quickly put a tape in the player. A second later the eerie howling

Marvin and Sarah had heard that night in the kitchen echoed through the house.

Mr. Wolfe's house was bursting with neighborhood children and parents. By now everyone had heard about the amazing robots and had come to see for themselves. Mr. Wolfe had become a neighborhood celebrity.

Marvin remained silent while Mr. Wolfe passed out more candy. Mr. Wolfe's reluctance to let the twins see the basement was clear now. Obviously that was his workroom. And the robots sitting around the room had been the feet and body Sarah had seen from the basement window.

"How did you make that tape?" Marvin asked when Mr. Wolfe finally had a chance to sit down. "It sounds almost real."

Mr. Wolfe chuckled. "Most of it is." He pointed to Jack, who was eagerly sniffing the robots, his tail waving in little circles. "Jack is a beagle. And if there is one thing beagles like to do, it's howl at the moon. I just dubbed in a few extra side effects."

"Which one is Henry?" Sarah asked, looking around the room.

Mr. Wolfe shook his head. "Well, my dear," he said to Miss Sweet, "I think it's time to introduce Henry."

TWENTY-ONE

Here's HENRY

Marvin glanced uneasily at the door. Mr. Wolfe still might not prove to be the innocent toy maker he claimed to be. It would be nice to have a fast getaway . . . just in case. But Mr. Wolfe stood with his back to the door, blocking the way. Marvin gulped and sat tensely on one corner of the couch while Miss Sweet disappeared into another room.

"Miss Sweet told me about her job as a detective," said Mr. Wolfe. "We had a long talk this morning. I wondered if you had overheard me mention Henry that day in the parking lot. But I never dreamed our conversation sounded like a murder conspiracy.

"The man you overheard that day was Mr. McGreggor, my boss," continued Mr. Wolfe. "He was upset because he had already made a deal to sell Dracula for a lot of money. But Henry was my first attempt. He's still my favorite," he added as Miss Sweet came back in the room with a small boxy figure with pincers instead of hands. "I didn't have time to work on him, but Charlotte's father is a renowned expert on computers. He really does work at the college. He offered to help work out a few bugs. See what you think."

Mr. Wolfe turned to Henry. "This is my friend Marvin," he said.

A row of little lights began blinking on the robot's head. He rolled over to Marvin and held out a pincer. "How do you do, Marvin," the robot said in a polite, gravelly voice.

Smiling, Marvin shook the robot's hand. Then Mr. Wolfe introduced him to Sarah and Ernie.

"Can he do anything else?" Ernie asked.

The robot reached into a compartment on its side. "Would you like to play ball?" he asked. He threw a small rubber ball to Marvin and caught it in the pincers when Marvin tossed it back.

"Would you like a drink?" Henry asked as he reached for a glass on the table. But his pincers knocked it down. "Whoops," said Henry. His head bent down. "Sorry," Henry said in a sad little voice.

"That's all right, Henry," said Detective Sweet.

"I'm going to program him to do lots of other things," said Mr. Wolfe. "If you had a robot like this, what would you want him to do?"

"Homework!" Sarah answered immediately.

"Take out the trash," Ernie suggested.

"Help me investigate mysteries" was Marvin's idea.

Mr. Wolfe chuckled. "I'm afraid such a clever robot would be too expensive for parents to buy."

"Hey," Sarah said suddenly. "If we don't get going, trick-or-treating will be over."

"Thanks for showing us Henry," Marvin said.

"Maybe someday you'll see a robot like Henry in the stores," said Mr. Wolfe.

"I hope so," Ernie answered.

"Good-bye, Marvin. Good-bye, Ernie. Good-bye, Sarah," Henry said, waving his pincers.

"Wow. Henry was great, wasn't he?" Ernie said as they hurried to the next house.

Marvin nodded. "I feel kind of dumb thinking Mr. Wolfe was a werewolf," he confessed.

"Jeepers," Sarah exclaimed. "Me too. And all the time he was just a nice toy maker."

"I think you're a great detective anyway," Ernie said loyally. "It was you who figured out about Frankie."

They arrived home an hour later with their bags bulging with candy. All along the way other trick-or-treaters had been talking about the scary monster house.

"Did you know what Mr. Wolfe was doing?" Sarah asked while Mr. and Mrs. Fremont checked their candy.

Mrs. Fremont nodded. "Mr. Wolfe invited me to look at the way the living room was set up. He wanted to be sure it wasn't too scary for the neighborhood children."

"We were afraid Mr. Wolfe was a werewolf," Sarah confessed. When her mother looked at her strangely, she added with an embarrassed glance, "I mean, with all the weird noises and all."

Mr. Fremont chuckled. "I thought you knew there was no such thing."

"Well, we do now," Marvin said. "From now on I'm going to concentrate on real criminals. Tomorrow I'm going to go to the post office and look at all the wanted posters."

"I'll go with you," Ernie said. "A good detective needs a bodyguard. Or," he added with a grin when Marvin looked at him, "a friend."

"Or a photographer," added Sarah.

"I think we've had enough detective work for now," said Mrs. Fremont. "Perhaps Marvin and Company should find a new hobby."

"Marvin and Company," said Marvin. "I like it."

Marvin the Magnificent and his new partners went upstairs to prepare for their next case.

Later that night, long after Ernie had gone home and Marvin and Sarah were tucked in bed, Mr. Wolfe looked out his window. The streets were dark and quiet. The last trick-or-treater was safely at home, stuffed with Halloween goodies, and Detective Sweet had driven away in her blue car. "What a fun night," he said to no one in particular. "I love Halloween." He studied the moon thoughtfully. "It's too bad it wasn't a full moon tonight. I always feel good when there is a full moon." Mr. Wolfe carried his robots one by one back down to his basement room—all except Dracula. Mr. Wolfe left him sitting on the living room couch. By the time he finished, Mr. Wolfe was panting. He opened his window and stood breathing in the cool night air.

Suddenly a giant bat swooped through the window and out into the night. Mr. Wolfe watched until the bat was only a tiny ghostly shape against the moon. "Good night, my friend," he called as he waved with one hairy hand—one very hairy hand.